SAVING THE PLANET
and Other Stories

SAVING THE PLANET

and Other Stories

THEODORE DALRYMPLE

MIRABEAU PRESS

Published by Mirabeau Press

PO Box 4281

West Palm Beach, FL 33401

ISBN: 978-1-7357055-2-1

First Edition

MIRABEAU

CONTENTS

SAVING THE PLANET

Like all middle-class girls, Arabella was exceptionally clever. Her cleverness did not prevent her from being either sweet or pretty, of course: she was both, exceptionally so. In short, she was perfect, and her parents, Julian and Francesca, foresaw a brilliant future for her.

They did not, as some parents do, live vicariously through their child or project onto her an unfulfilled ambition of their own. They did not need to, for their own careers had been more than successful. Julian was a political journalist and restaurant critic who appeared from time to time on television, while Francesca was an interior decorator à la mode. They lived in a world in which money was a problem only if you had been exceptionally foolish: they had all that they could reasonably have wished to have. Julian had written a book on the harmful effects of the motor car which had sold very well, and Francesca did not lack for clients. They had an interesting circle of friends, unsurprisingly rather like themselves. Any disagreements at dinner parties were on details rather than matters of principle, which were settled and never very great. The art on their walls, abstract, was cool and soothing. Their maid and nanny, a Filipina called Maria, was invariably smiling and helpful and lived in a light and airy basement that was almost a flat of its own.

Thanks to the nature of their work, Julian and Francesca were able to take several holidays a year. They went to places like the rain forests of Costa Rica or the Okavango Swamps, though they also took weekends in Venice: thus, they combined Art and Nature.

Francesca had worked to establish herself before she had a child and was thirty-five when Arabella was born. But people in their forties these days were not even middle-aged; it would not even be accurate to say that Francesca had aged well, but rather that she had reached a long period of agelessness in which change was almost inconceivable. She didn't have to buy face-creams or anything of that nature to hide the ravages of time.

Julian and Francesca adored Arabella, of course, and were proud of her. They compared her with other children of her age, employing only objective criteria. Oddly enough, several of their women friends had had children at almost the same time as Arabella had been born: it was, if you thought about it, a very curious coincidence. But Arabella was clearly the brightest of her contemporaries and asked such penetrating questions that all who knew her grew used to her precocity. Obviously, she absorbed information like a sponge and reflected on it deeply. Not that she was all thought and no play: she loved climbing trees fearlessly, for example, laughing at her parents' anxiety. She was a leader among her friends and enjoyed dressing up, as a fairy for example. Then she would wave her magic wand, which had a glittery star at the top, and order her friends about, being not just a fairy but Queen of the Fairies. And they obeyed her.

Although they always dressed casually, almost as a matter of principle, Julian and Francesca loved to see Arabella in the Kittiwake House school uniform. She looked adorable in her green blazer with yellow piping, and her straw boater with a ribbon of the same colours. And Arabella liked her uniform too; she was not one of those children who became a mess as soon as she escaped from parental oversight. When Francesca picked her up from school in her shining, new, four-wheel drive vehicle, she always looked almost as neat and perfect as she had when she arrived. Francesca's heart swelled with pride and love as she watched her clamber up into the back seat of the vehicle and put on her safety-belt without having to be told to do so. On the way home, Arabella would chatter gaily about all she had done or learnt in school that day. Francesca never had any difficulty getting her ready for school. On the contrary, Arabella was always as eager to go to school as was Felix, their golden retriever, to go for a walk.

Julian and Francesca had thought it would be good for Arabella to be brought up with a dog; in that way she would learn to like, and above all respect, animals. And Arabella did love Felix: she would wrap her arms around his neck and kiss and hug him (of course, his deworming was up to date). Felix was infinitely patient with her, as he had been earlier when, much younger, she had pulled his tail like a rope. It was as if he understood that there was no malice in it, that she was still a very young child and would grow out of it. Fortunately, Arabella was not the kind of child who needed to be told many times not to do something.

Despite always coming top of her class, Arabella was popular with the other girls. Her superiority and leadership were not deliberate but natural and effortless. The other girls obeyed her wishes or suggestions as she obeyed the wishes or suggestions of her parents. Her head was not swollen, as some girls' heads might have been swollen by such pre-eminence. She incited no enemies and provoked no envy.

The school year came to an end, and Arabella, as did all her class, moved up into the year above. After the long summer holiday, she returned eagerly to Kittiwake House, for even she had begun to tire of finding something to do for herself. Her class teacher was no longer Miss Jones. The Headmistress of Kittiwake House thought it was unhealthy for the girls to grow too attached to a particular teacher and good for them to be exposed to more than one. It would gently help them to learn about the complexity of the world and human beings and how to adapt to it.

Ms Green was new to the school: it was her first term of teaching there. She wore black-rimmed, rectangular spectacles with such small lenses that it could not have been at all easy to look though them. Her black hair fell about her face in ringlets which shook a little when she spoke, as if to emphasise what she said. She had a broad mouth full of teeth like the white keys of a piano. She had a metal bangle round her right wrist which slid up and down slightly when she wrote on the blackboard. Her clothes were of thin cotton patterned in an unusual, semi-African way and her shoes appeared to be of a kind of tough straw woven closely together.

Francesca asked Arabella what she thought of her new teacher after the first day in her new class. Had she liked her?

Did she like her as much as she had liked Miss Jones?

'She said you mustn't call her Miss Jones,' said Arabella.

'No? Why not?' asked her mother.

'You must call her Ms Jones.'

'Why did she say that?'

'She said Miss was a bad word.'

'Bad? Bad in what way?'

'She said it was a word they used a long time ago when girls weren't allowed to be anything important.'

Francesca laughed. It was true that calling Miss Jones Miss was behind the times. Perhaps it was just as well that Ms Green insisted now, while Arabella was so young, so that she did not have to learn later, when it might be confusing to her. And at least Ms Green would not put any implicit psychological obstacle in Arabella's way, inhibiting her choice of career from the outset. Of course, it was early days to be thinking about such things, but at least Arabella would experience none of the mind-forged manacles that had impeded so many girls in their time.

'So you won't call anybody Miss anymore?' asked Francesca, smiling.

'No,' said Arabella, with the earnestness of the very young when saying something very important.

Arabella settled into her new class without mentioning any difficulty. She didn't complain of anything, but somehow her brow was now often furrowed, as if she were worrying over something. She seemed almost distracted when Francesca read her a story at night. Reading her a story was the least Francesca could do, considering how guiltily absent she was from Arabella's life most of the time, apart from fetching her to and carrying her from school every day.

'Arabella, darling,' she asked her one night, 'is there anything bothering you?'

'No, mummy,' she replied, but not quite spontaneously. She stared intensely into the bedclothes.

'Are you sure? There's no one bullying you? No one's stealing your things?'

'No, mummy.'

'You would tell me if there were, wouldn't you, darling?'

'Yes, mummy.'

Francesca was relieved, even though Arabella's frown had not quite dispersed.

'Anyway, Ms Green says we should share everything,' Arabella added. 'She says we must learn to share everything.'

'And so you must, darling,' said Francesca, laughing. 'You don't want to grow up to be a selfish young woman, do you?'

'No, mummy. Ms Green says that being selfish is very wicked.'

'She's quite right.'

'She said that selfish people rule the world.'

'Well…' said Francesca. Of course, it was true in a way; no one could really deny it. Francesca had often found that suppliers, sub-contractors and clients would swindle you if they could, not all of them, of course, but at least some of them, and not necessarily those with the least money. Only that day the Davenports had tried to lower the price of what she had done by claiming some footling deviation from the initial design which, moreover, had been forced on her by circumstances. They should have been grateful to her, rather than try to chisel her out of fifteen per cent. In the end, she had had to agree; otherwise they would have made her wait interminably for even the reduced sum. Sometimes she wondered why she bothered. After all, Julian earned more than enough for both of them. She supposed she must have liked what she was doing.

'Selfish people are not usually very happy,' said Francesca. She and Julian had decided that when Arabella raised awkward questions (which all children of any intelligence do) they would never lie to her, even if there were aspects of the truth that had, for the moment, to be hidden or disguised. Besides, it was true that selfish people were not usually very happy.

'Why aren't they very happy, mummy?' asked Arabella.

'Because they are always thinking of themselves, never of anybody else,' said Francesca. 'That's why nobody loves them. They keep everything for themselves. Would you like to go to a birthday party where the birthday girl wouldn't share any of her cake?'

'Then why do selfish people rule the world, mummy, if no one likes them, just like Ms Green says?'

Francesca looked at her watch.

'Goodness, Arabella, darling,' she said. 'It's well past your bedtime. It's time for you to go to sleep, or you'll be too tired to go to school in the morning, and you wouldn't like that, would you?'

'No, mummy.' She shut her eyes like a good girl, as if sleep could be conjured at will. 'I'll try not to be selfish,' she murmured, and then indeed she did fall asleep.

Arabella went no less willingly to school than before but went now with a more serious expression on her face, as if school were more than just fun, which it had always been before. This was odd, because in point of discipline Miss Jones had been far more severe than Ms Green. Miss Jones would insist that the children sat still at their desks facing the front, at least for most of the time, but Ms Green arranged the classroom is if it were a restaurant and she were the head waitress, asking the children what they would like today. But despite this, Arabella took on the air of a perpetually worried little girl.

Francesca spoke to Julian about it. She asked him, 'Have you noticed anything about Arabella these days?'

'What about her?' Julian was particularly busy and absorbed currently because there was a political crisis greater than usual, and he was constantly being asked for his prognosis. Would the government survive? Who might succeed the Prime Minister if he fell? Would there be an election, and if so who would win it? What was the likely effect of the crisis on the economy? He had even been on television three nights in succession, on one occasion speaking for two minutes uninterruptedly.

'She's changed,' said Francesca. 'She's worried all the time, ever since she changed class at school.'

'I hadn't noticed.'

Of course he hadn't: too preoccupied to notice. Even when he was less busy than now, he buried himself in books. General preparation, he called it by way of excuse. Francesca decided to speak to Maria. After all, she had more contact with Arabella than anybody. So later that day, while Julian was dealing with the political crisis, Francesca called Maria into the dining room and sat her down at the large, slightly heavy,

8

William IV dining table.

'Maria,' she said, 'have you noticed anything wrong with Arabella these days?'

Maria's eyes darted furtively round the room. She looked as though she thought she was being accused of something which would be a reason to dismiss her. Then she would lose her work permit and be deported back to the Philippines. If she returned to her parents, they would pressure her once again to marry Gonzalo, the boy who had wooed her, and more than wooed her, leaving her with child. But if she lost her job and didn't go back, how would she keep herself?

'No, madame,' she said, trying to affect surprise.

'Are you sure? She doesn't cry when she's with you or alone, or anything like that?'

'No, madame.'

She called Francesca madame whenever she was nervous. Francesca had the impression, therefore, that she was hiding something from her, but there was little chance of discovering what. She had the devious obstinacy of the perpetually subservient.

A few days later, Arabella returned home from school with her mother as usual. Felix, the retriever, came as enthusiastically as ever to greet her. He picked up his rubber goose in his mouth and twirled round madly in ever-decreasing circles, then running after mother and daughter and bumping into them in order to be stroked. Normally, Arabella would have put her arms round Felix's neck and given him a hug, but today she did not. Instead, she took a step back as if in horror or disgust. Francesca noticed.

'Whatever is the matter, darling?' asked Francesca. 'Is there something wrong with Felix?'

Arabella remained silent.

'Arabella, what is it? What's wrong, darling?'

'Ms Green says it's wrong to keep animals.'

Francesca was startled. Felix was such a nice dog, even the postman wasn't frightened of him.

'Why does she say it's wrong to keep animals?'

'She says it's cruel.'

'Cruel! But Arabella, darling, we love Felix, don't we? And he loves us. He has his toys just like you, and he always comes with us when we go to the park.'

'Ms Green says that animals should have their own lives. She says they shouldn't be pets at all.'

'Don't be silly, darling. Felix has a very nice life. If I had a second life after I die, I would like to come back as Felix.'

'Ms Green says that animals should be free, not locked up.' There was a slight hard edge to Arabella's tone which Francesca had never noticed before.

'But think, Arabella, darling. What would poor Felix do without us? He'd never survive on his own. Who would feed him, who would cuddle him?'

By this time, Felix was desperate for an embrace and couldn't understand why he hadn't had one. He bumped into them ever more desperately, reminding them of his due. Francesca went down on one knee and cuddled him almost fiercely, to demonstrate to Arabella what she should do. Felix licked her face.

'See how he loves us,' said Francesca. 'If we were cruel to him, would he do that?'

'Ms Green says that pets are prisoners.'

'Well, not everything that Ms Green says…' She held herself back at the last moment. Julian and she had agreed from the beginning that they would back each other up in front of Arabella, even if they thought each other in the wrong, in order to maintain their authority in Arabella's eyes. Ms Green was an extension of parental authority, so to speak, and Arabella was now old and clever enough to exploit any cracks in it, and to divide and rule. And Ms Green was going to be Arabella's teacher for almost a year.

Felix nudged Arabella. She stroked him gingerly at first, as if he might be dangerous and turn on her, but then she gave into her natural feelings for him and hugged him. Francesca was relieved.

'See how he loves us?' she said. Everything was back to normal.

That evening, Francesca spoke to Julian, but his mind was on other things. A minister had just resigned because he had used an air force helicopter to take him to a flower show in the company of a woman 'not his wife', as one newspaper delicately put it. His wife had issued a press statement saying that she was sticking by him. Divorce would come later, said Julian, laughing.

'I think Ms Green's been putting ideas into Arabella's head,' said Francesca.

'Ms Green, who's Ms Green?' asked Julian.

'Don't be silly, darling,' replied Francesca, her forced lightness of tone not altogether concealing her irritation. 'She's Arabella's class teacher.'

'Ah yes, of course.'

'She's been putting ideas into Arabella's head.'

'Isn't that what she's paid to do?'

'Not those kind of ideas. She's been telling Arabella that keeping pets like Felix is wrong, so when we came back today from school, she wouldn't hug him at first like she normally does. I had to persuade her to.'

'But she did in the end?'

'Yes, of course, she loves Felix.'

'Well then, it doesn't really matter what Ms Green says, does it? In fact, Ms Green is doing her job as a teacher. She sets Arabella thinking. And she came to her own conclusion, which is good.'

'She's too young. It'll make her anxious if what she wants to do is different from what she's told she ought to do.'

'That's what life's like,' said Julian. 'And the sooner she learns to think for herself, the better.'

The necessity to think for oneself was one of Julian's favourite themes. It was why he had always worked independently, why he would never have been able to ascend any hierarchy of which he was part.

Francesca could tell, though, that his mind was not really on the subject. When his mind was on something other than what was being talked about, in this case the government crisis — he had said in an article that it wasn't so much a question of this or that minister but of trust in our whole system — he issued perfunctory statements without any real thought or feeling behind them.

A few days later, Arabella returned from school very excited.

'Mummy,' she said, 'Ms Green showed us something funny today.'

'What was it, darling?'

'She rolled up her sleeve, and there was a dragon on her arm.'

A dragon? A tattoo, of course.

'She said it kept her safe.'

Safe? Safe from what? Surely there could be few safer occupations in the world than teacher at Kittiwake House School?

'Safe from what, darling?' asked Francesca.

'From all the bad things,' replied Arabella.

'What bad things?'

'All bad things. Ms Green said there were bad things everywhere, especially when we can't see them.'

Francesca would have to have another talk with Julian about Ms Green.

'Mummy,' Arabella asked, with a slight wheedle in her voice, 'can I have a dragon on my arm like Ms Green?'

Francesca was horrified.

'Certainly not, darling, no!' She spoke more sharply than perhaps she might have wished and regretted it.

'Why can't I have one?'

'Because you're far too young, Arabella.' Though broadminded, Francesca detested tattoos. 'Perhaps you can have one when you're older.'

'When I'm ten?', asked Arabella eagerly.

'No, when you're much older than that.'

'When I'm twelve?'

'We'll see.' There was no point in giving her an unimaginable distant age to look forward to. She would soon forget all about it anyway.

Arabella frowned, pouted and sulked, and she would have stamped her feet if her feet had reached the floor from the seat of the vehicle in which they were travelling together.

'It's not fair,' she said.

Julian and Francesca had decided long ago that, whenever possible, they would reason with Arabella rather than merely exert their authority.

'What's not fair, darling?' said Francesca.

'Ms Green can have a dragon, and I can't.'

'Ms Green is an adult,' said Francesca. 'Much older than you.'

'I can't help being a child.'

'Adults are allowed things that children aren't.'

'Why?'

'Because that's how it is,' said Francesca, making a difficult left turn into a street almost too narrow for the car. That, and the fact that attempts at reasoning with Arabella always ended with assertions of authority anyway, irritated her.

After Arabella was tucked up in bed and asleep (as far as Francesca could tell), she went to Julian who was working in his study. The government crisis was deepening: it had been discovered that a minister had signed a consulting agreement with a supply company to take effect when he left office.

'It's Ms Green again,' she said. 'Did you know she's tattooed?'

'No. So what?'

'She showed it in class today.'

'I'm sure the girls must have been very interested.'

'Now Arabella wants one. She asked me whether she could have one.'

'Children are like that. They want something for a time and then they forget it.'

'That's not the point.'

'What is the point?'

'Ms Green frightened her. She said her tattoo, which was of a dragon, protected her from all the bad things.'

'What bad things?'

'That's it, she didn't say. She made the children think that they were surrounded by dangers which have to be warded off.'

'Well, aren't there? What are vaccinations for except to ward off dangers? And don't we try to teach her road safety?'

'That's different,' said Francesca, growing irritated by Julian. 'Those dangers are real. I'm worried that Ms Green is trying to frighten the children in general.'

'In what way?'

Francesca had difficulty in explaining.

'She is trying to persuade her that the world is full of unseen hazards.'

'Like viruses?'

'Viruses are real, physical. No, I mean things evil.'

'Like witches and ghosts?'

'Yes, something like that.'

'Children like being frightened. Look at all their fairy stories: they're full of witches and the like. You can't get much scarier than the Brothers Grimm.'

'That's different. And anyway, I don't read Grimm to Arabella just before she goes to sleep.'

'Neither does Ms Green.'

Julian could be very obtuse when it suited him. He was very

intelligent, of course, even brilliant, but when he didn't want to think about something, he always found a good way to divert attention from it. That was the problem with intelligence: you could misuse it. Francesca knew that what he was really thinking about all the while was his wretched political crisis. Things nearer home simply didn't interest him. The further away they were from him, the more important to him they seemed. When he was in a mood like this, it was useless to continue. You might as well preach to a plank of wood.

Arabella grew ever more serious; at least, she wore a perpetual frown on her face. One day, she threw Jemima, her favourite doll, into the non-organic waste bin in the kitchen. She did it with a flourish, almost angrily. She wanted her mother to notice what she had done.

'Arabella, darling, what are you doing? That's Jemima you're throwing in the bin.'

'Stupid Jemima! Stupid, stupid Jemima! She's useless.'

'But you've always loved Jemima.'

'No, I don't, not anymore. I'm a big girl now. I'm almost a woman. Women don't have dolls.'

'Ha!' Francesca's little exclamation was devoid of mirth. Actually, she had a soft, little stuffed elephant on her bed. 'Who put that idea into your head?'

Of course, she already knew the answer.

'Ms Green. She said dolls were wrong anyway.'

'And why are dolls wrong?'

'They're stupid. They prevent us from growing up like boys.'

Arabella could not be persuaded to rescue Jemima from the

bin. As far as she was concerned, Jemima was now where she ought to be and ought always to have been. She said that all the other girls in her class were throwing away their dolls, too. Only a few months before, Arabella had begged and begged Francesca to buy Jemima for her, as if it had been the most urgent thing in the world. Arabella had thought of nothing else for several weeks, as, apparently, had many of her friends.

The episode was the occasion of another unsatisfactory consultation with Julian. He did not take seriously the almost violent disposal of the doll. He remembered from his childhood his own sudden abandonment of marbles and conkers, which until that moment had seemed of supreme importance.

'Children grow out of things,' he said.

Julian was determined to see no problems, because problems were an inconvenience, a distraction.

Two weeks later, Arabella refused to get into the car to go to school. She was very stubborn about it, her face set in an expression of determination. At first, Francesca thought she must be frightened of something.

'Get into the car, darling,' she said. 'We're late. There's nothing to be frightened of.'

But Arabella was like Felix when, out for a walk, he didn't want to be pulled away from the base of a tree whose odour he found particularly alluring. Arabella refused to move.

'I'll get cross in a moment,' said Francesca. 'It's getting later and later.'

It was, too. Francesca had a meeting scheduled with a client just after dropping Arabella off at school. It was inconvenient: she had barely enough time, but the client, a biggish businessman, had insisted on that time and no other. It was amazing how rich clients had an unfailing instinct for causing inconvenience. And so, apparently, now had Arabella — she, who had never been reluctant before to go to school. Francesca felt a mounting anxiety mixed with anger.

'Get in the car,' she said with some asperity.

'No,' said Arabella. 'I'm not going to.'

'Why not?' asked Francesca, just managing to control her urge to lift Arabella bodily into the car.

'I'm not going to go to school in a car anymore,' said Arabella. Her statement had a tone of finality about it that was impressive for one so young.

'Arabella, stop playing around. We're late already. Get into the car.'

'Ms Green says that cars are bad, especially big ones. Hers is very small and she uses it only when she absolutely has to. She says we should walk to school or come on the bus.'

Ms Green says this, Ms Green says that! Francesca was growing a trifle weary of Ms Green.

'For the last time, Arabella, get in the car!' and she gave her daughter a little push in the back.

Arabella, realising that she would be unequal to any real struggle, reluctantly did as she was told, with a pout that she wanted her mother to see.

'Now what's all this about Ms Green?' asked Francesca once they were on their way.

'She says that if we go about in cars, soon we won't be able to breathe.'

'Nonsense,' Francesca snapped. 'She's putting ideas into your head.'

'She says it's selfish to go about in cars which are mostly empty. Cars need more and more roads, and they cover up all the grass and the fields where flowers grow.'

'Oh really!' said Francesca, halfway between exasperation and sarcastic interrogative.

'And she says there won't be any more bees and worms,' continued Arabella confidently. 'We did earthworms last week, before they all disappear.'

'They're not going to disappear.' Just then, an angry driver sounded his horn and shook his fist at Francesca because she had cut across his path.

'Earthworms can't live under roads,' said Arabella. She was quite categorical about this. 'And if there are roads everywhere, there won't be any worms. And if there are no worms, there won't be any soil. And if there isn't any soil, nothing will grow and there won't be anything to eat.'

Francesca braked just in time to avoid a cyclist.

'Why can't they look where they're going?' she said testily.

'That's why we mustn't go in cars when we don't have to,' resumed Arabella, her train of thought unbroken by the near-accident.

'Damn!' said Francesca when the lights ahead turned red.

'That's why we should walk to school or go by bicycle. Though walking's better,' added Arabella definitively.

'And why's that?' asked Francesca.

'Because bicycles have to be made, and they have a lot of metal in them.'

'And why is that bad?'

'Because metal has to be dug out of the ground, and it makes a lot of smoke.'

In the days following, Arabella made such a scene about getting into the car that Francesca gave in and henceforth they walked to school. Because of the traffic, in fact, it took only twenty minutes longer and wasn't in itself unpleasant. But Arabella agreed to be taken home in the car because she was tired after school. Francesca resolved that Julian and she would have to have a word with Ms Green.

Of course, when she first told Julian about Ms Green and Arabella's refusal to get in the car, he had said, 'They're right in a way. It is an absurdly large car for what you need it for. Imagine what it would be like if everyone had one like it.'

Sometimes, Francesca thought, Julian was still like an adolescent trying to shock his parents: he took a contrary position just for the sake of it. What had seemed amusing when she first knew him had become merely tiresome.

They nevertheless went to see Ms Green, by appointment, one school lunchbreak. They discovered that she was quite pretty, though Francesca didn't like the little gold stud in one side of her nose and the ring in the top of her left ear. She was surprised that the headmistress of Kittiwake House School permitted such adornment in her teachers, but perhaps she had little choice. Ms Green, though, was well-spoken and perfectly polite, even welcoming.

Francesca was determined to be unfriendly and grimly direct; one might almost say aggressive.

'Ever since you told Arabella that cars were bad,' she said, 'she's refused to be driven to school.'

Ms Green smiled sweetly.

'I don't tell my students anything,' she said. 'It's not my way. I give them facts and encourage them to think for themselves. If Arabella doesn't want to be driven in a car, it's her idea, not mine. I must admit, however, that if she's come to that conclusion herself, I'm proud of her.'

'She wouldn't have thought of it if you hadn't set her thinking.'

'Isn't that the point of education?' piped up Julian, taking Ms Green's side, though he had been slightly surprised to hear her call Arabella a student rather than a pupil.

Francesca shot him an angry look. He wasn't helping at all, just the reverse. He was obviously flirting with Ms Green, trying to make himself look clever and amusing in her eyes, a free spirit unlike his wife. Free spirit! It was she who had the overwhelming part in Arabella's upbringing — except, perhaps, for Maria, the rigid Catholic. It was a mistake to have brought Julian to the meeting, but she had wanted to show Ms Green that Arabella had two parents whose views were not lightly to be brushed aside. Instead, Ms Green had found an ally in Julian.

'Arabella should be taught to read, write and do arithmetic,' said Francesca, surprised at her own opinion.

'Arabella already does those things,' said Ms Green. 'In fact, she does them very well, much better than average for her age. She has an inquiring mind.'

'She shouldn't at her age be worrying about things like pollution… and other things that will worry her.'

'I don't teach her those things,' said Ms Green. 'I ask the girls a few questions, that's all, and let them develop their thoughts. They have to learn about the world they live in. After all, it's going to be theirs longer than it's going to be ours.'

It was strange to hear Ms Green speak like this because she was still in her twenties.

'I asked the girls to write four pages about what they liked and didn't like about cars, and then we discussed their answers in class.'

The bell rang for the end of the lunchbreak. Ms Green said that she had to go: the children were wating for her.

On the way home, Francesca said to Julian, 'Ms Green's intimidating Arabella.'

Julian laughed lightly. 'No, she's not,' he said. 'You heard what she told us. She just gets the children to think for themselves.'

'And think precisely what she thinks. She's a fanatic.'

'No, she's not. Look how she dresses. Fanatics don't dress like that.'

'I think we should consider taking Arabella away from Kittiwake House.'

'That'd be awful for her. She's settled there, all her friends are there.'

'How would you know? You never take any interest in what she's doing at school.'

'I read her reports. She's always top of her class. She wouldn't be if she were unhappy. I don't think we should upset the apple cart.'

'That's just because you can't be bothered to look for another school. It would bore you.'

'I'm just thinking of Arabella.'

'You're thinking of your precious political situation so that you can write your articles,' said Francesca bitterly. 'That's all you ever care about.'

There was silence between them the rest of the way home. It wasn't merely the absence of sound but the presence of hostility. By tacit consent, they tried to hide it from Arabella.

The following Sunday, they sat down together for lunch. There was roast chicken.

'I don't want any,' said Arabella, with a tone of finality.

'Why not, darling?' asked Arabella, her heart sinking, and dreading what was to come. 'You love chicken.'

'I did love chicken,' replied Arabella. 'But Ms Green says we shouldn't eat meat. The way chickens are kept is cruel.'

'But all our chickens are free-range,' said Francesca. 'I always make sure of that. It means that they can run around and have a happy life before we eat them.'

'And they taste better,' said Julian, unhelpfully.

'The way they're killed is terrible,' said Arabella. She spoke almost as if she had rehearsed what she had to say.

'Chickens aren't like us, darling,' said Francesca. 'They don't feel much, so they can't suffer. It's not like when you're ill.'

'And Ms Green says that for each chicken you could grow enough food to feed ten families in Africa.'

Francesca kept her temper, but only just.

'We're not in Africa, dear, we're in England.'

'But we could send the food there and save their babies.'

'And what would we eat?'

'The same as them. We could eat plants. Ms Brown says that we could easily grow enough food for the whole world so that no one would have to go hungry.'

'But you need to eat meat to grow,' said Francesca.

'Ms Green says you can get all you need to grow from

plants.'

'It's very difficult.'

'She says she does it. And it's healthier.'

'I'll have to have a word again with Ms Green,' said Francesca, and put some chicken on Arabella's plate.

'I don't want it,' said Arabella firmly. 'It's disgusting. I won't eat it.'

'Just eat the vegetables,' said Julian, trying to smooth things over. 'Leave the chicken if you don't want it.'

'They've touched the chicken,' said Arabella, 'so they've got meat on them now.'

She wouldn't eat even the vegetables until they had been dished out on a clean plate. She was an obstinate girl, and when she spoke, she stared straight ahead, as if not addressing anyone in particular.

'I want lentils,' she said. 'Ms Green says they're good for you and good for the planet.'

From then on, Arabella would eat no meat or fish and would clamp her mouth shut in its presence.

'It's intolerable,' said Francesca to Julian, 'Ms Green forcing us to live this way.'

'It's commonplace these days,' said Julian. 'I was reading only the other day that a third of girls and a quarter of boys are now vegetarian.'

'That's not the point,' said Francesca. 'I'm going to move Arabella away from Kittiwake House whether you like it or not.'

Francesca began to make enquiries about nearby schools. All of them were flawed. One was too religious, another taught no French. She had still found none to her liking when

Arabella made another announcement, as if she were the spokesman for some important organisation.

'I'm not eating any more eggs,' she said, 'or drinking any more milk. And I'm not wearing any leather shoes.' Her face was set like a rock.

Francesca slammed a cup down on the table.

'I've had just about enough of Ms Green!' she said. 'And of your passivity,' she added, looking at Julian.

'It's not my fault if Ms Green's a harridan,' said Julian.

'Harridan? I'm not talking about her being a harridan. It's not because she's a woman. It would be the same if she were a man.'

'But she isn't,' said Julian.

A week later, with Arabella still eating no eggs and drinking no milk, Francesca unceremoniously put her in the car and did up her seatbelt.

'We're not going to school today,' she said. 'We're going on holiday. Daddy's not coming with us. In fact, Daddy's not going to live with us anymore. We're going to live somewhere else from now on.'

Arabella looked at her mother.

'Ms Green says that daddies aren't needed,' she said. 'She says they're a nuisance.'

I, Being of Sound Mind

He was on his death bed, and he did not, as others did, disguise it from himself. All his life he had prided himself on his rationality, on facing things as they really were and not as he would have liked them to be. How could he now shy away from the small matter of death? Indeed, death had long been one of the favourite subjects of his secular sermons.

'Death,' he said, 'is a natural part of life, as natural as eating or drinking. Then what is there to be afraid of? Once you are dead, you are dead. There is no pie-in-the-sky when you're dead, and anyone who tells you different is a fraud and a deceiver who is trying to take advantage of you here below. No, there is nothing to be afraid of in death.'

Did he convert anybody from fear of death? He never thought about it: the point was to be right, not to be effective. His one slight regret was that there would be no one after his death to whom he could say, 'I told you so.'

Of course, death was not quite the end: there was the funeral to consider, and he considered it. This was no time not to face truths, and the fact is that, though he was not a believer, religious funerals were best. Non-religious funerals, he had observed, were awkward affairs, in which everyone was like a dancer with two left feet. The mourners, or attendees, hung about not quite knowing what to say to each other. The person conducting the service, or ceremony, or whatever you called it, was either a friend or relation who had never done anything like it before, or was a professional who adopted all the intonations of a clergyman at his soapiest, but who failed to hold out the false hope or consolation of some ghostly or attenuated survival of the recently departed. But in the light of the universe's fate as the apotheosis of the Second Law of Thermodynamics, what did it matter, he thought, if he betrayed his principles for once and directed that he should have a religious funeral? After all, the greatest happiness of the greatest number was what really mattered, and if his funeral would not really be a pleasure, at least it could avoid awkwardness for those few who would attend it.

But who would they be, and how many of them? These were important questions, for upon the answers depended how many sandwiches and other refreshments should be ordered for the collation afterwards. On the one hand, he reprehended waste, but on the other he did not want to appear miserly at the last. There was a delicate balance to be struck.

Who would come to the funeral? His three brothers, of course, though they detested him, and two of their wives, the third having died of the consequences of smoking of which he had warned her repeatedly, to which she had always airily replied that you had to die of something and in any case she knew someone in her nineties who had smoked fifty a day throughout her life and was in perfect health. What argument! Well, she had paid the price of her folly and died before her time. Actually, her death was all of a piece with her life, a long series of caprices and indiscretions that had caused her husband, his brother, nothing but grief. It had been obvious from the first what she was like, and he had told his brother not to marry her, but he hadn't listened. People, alas, have to make their own decisions.

His thoughts returned to the question of who would attend his funeral. There were his nephews and nieces, six of them, all hopeful of a legacy. Of course, by then it would be too late for him to alter his will in favour of any of them, so attendance was beside the point, but no doubt there were appearances to be preserved. He had no illusions about the degree of their affection for him or their reasons for visiting him. The only one he himself really liked was Lionel who, unusually for the family, was a little slow, his lack of intelligence preventing him from forming ulterior motives. What he lacked in ability, he made up for in character. He was smiling, docile, obedient and willing, just what was needed for help in the garden when he came to stay for a few weeks. He did what he was told and never answered back because he did not claim to know everything, unlike most young people nowadays who always knew everything. He had no initiative of his own, which meant that any mistakes that he made were those of execution rather than of design, and therefore small, easily rectified. He tried to follow instructions to the letter, and if he failed to do so, well, he could be forgiven because he was impaired by nature. He was much better than paid gardeners who always suffered from ideas of their own, which was where trouble began. They were obstinate and insisted on doing things their own way just because their way was theirs. They claimed to know how to deal with greenfly, for instance, when it was obvious that they didn't. Lionel was more use.

It had been just the same in the office, too. Young men of no experience would claim to know how to do things better, taking short-cuts in the name of efficiency. They had no sense of system or method and didn't pause to analyse problems in a logical fashion. When he sold his company, which he had founded with a loan from his brother (who was much less educated and articulate than he), to a much larger company, he discovered that they too had no sense of system or method. He had tried to tell them, but they wouldn't listen.

No, Lionel was useful, there was no other word for it: useful. It was his highest term of praise. There were so many useless people in the world! Once he had been co-opted on to a committee of the Board of Trade, as it was then called, and all that the other members of the committee could do was object to his ideas. Time-wasters, the lot of them! How any of them had built a business he couldn't imagine. They had only to open their mouths for sheer idiocies to emerge.

Lionel would come to the funeral, of course, brought by his father. At one time, he had left the bulk of his considerable estate to Lionel as the most deserving of his relatives, but he had subsequently changed his mind, as he always did after making a will. 'I, being of sound mind' he had written, 'hereby bequeath...'

He was too mean to employ a lawyer to draw up his wills — thieves, the lot of them — and he had learned that something on a scrap of paper would do, provided it was authentic. He chuckled at the thought of the legal challenges that they would all bring after his death, claiming that this or that of his wills was the real one, depending on whom it benefitted most. They would claim that all subsequent wills were invalid, written under undue influence, or some such impediment. Bogus arguments, of course, but grist to any lawyer's mill. With luck, the proceedings would be so long, involved and costly that they would eat up the estate entirely.

Of course, he had always let them all know what was in his latest will; there was no point in hiding his light under a bushel. It kept them on their toes, and it kept them visiting him when he knew that they did not want to. It made them civil if not affectionate. When he told them that he was leaving everything to Lionel, 'in consideration of his faithful service and help in the garden' as he put it in the document, he knew that they were scandalised. Oh yes, he knew what they were thinking all right: 'What the hell is a mentally handicapped boy with a mental age of ten going to do with all that money? All he wants is bags of sweets.'

He changed his mind, however, as he always did. If he left everything to Lionel, they would get their hands on it one way or another unless, that is, he set up some kind of trust, and then the trustees would loot it. But the threat of leaving everything to Lionel was a shot across their bows: they would have to take him seriously if they hoped for anything.

However, in all subsequent wills he left Lionel a cut glass bowl from the dining room which he had always liked because of the way, if he moved his head a little, he saw little rainbows coming out of it.

Only one of his two sons would come to the funeral, the other, Simon, having left the country to live as far away as possible. He had wanted to be an artist – pah! Romantic nonsense. As a father, it had been his duty to steer him away from the precarious and impoverished life of an artist, or at any rate of the overwhelming majority of artists. No doubt there were one or two who made fortunes, but to embark on a career in the hope of becoming one of a tiny elite was like buying a lottery ticket and expecting to win, which was completely irrational. He had told Simon that he wouldn't pay for him to go to art school but would support him if he chose to study something that would bring him a steady income for the rest of his life, such as accountancy. The young fool had run away in a rage, when he had only been trying to make him see sense. He had been obliged to take menial jobs on the other side of the world just to keep himself and of course had never become an artist, as he would have done had he had a true vocation. Artist, indeed! Nothing would have stopped him if he had any talent. Imagine what Rembrandt would have done if his father had tried to prevent hm from becoming an artist. He would have become an artist anyway. Now his son was just a minor official in a government office, the acme of his achievement being a pension.

Nevertheless, in one of his wills he left everything to Simon. This disposition of his worldly goods did not last long, but long enough to alarm his brother, Geoffrey, who thought that he deserved the universal legacy instead. He would come to the funeral, the hypocritical creep. It wasn't difficult to see through him! He had followed his father's advice about a career, mainly out of cowardice, so that at least as a result he hadn't had any financial problems, but on the other hand his wife was intolerable hysteric, the exact opposite, almost, of his own cautious and pusillanimous character. She was skittish, inconstant, grasping and spendthrift. She would be able to run through any amount of money with nothing to show for it. That would have been amusing to observe: the vicious arguments between them that her incontinent wastefulness would have occasioned.

He had stirred their avarice by letting it be known that he was thinking for a time of leaving everything to her husband, Geoffrey. Their visits to him grew a little more frequent than before, and she brought with her home-made jam as a gift, 'a little token,' as she put it. He tried it, deliberating over it as a real oenophile deliberates over the finest vintages.

'It's very good' he said at last, after rational reflection, 'but I think that it needs just a little touch of acidity,' and went to fetch a lemon to squeeze into it.

Her expression was a rictus rather than a smile. The love of money, he thought to himself, is not only the root of all evil, but, in a case like hers, of all self-control. She didn't normally fail to rise to his bait, but now she didn't want to do anything to spoil the chances of the legacy. In other circumstances she would have said, 'Why can't you just say it's very good, and leave it at that?,' to which he would have replied, 'It's my honest opinion, and if I didn't tell you what I really thought, how could you improve?'

At least she wouldn't require many sandwiches, for among her many bad or irritating qualities was an obsession with remaining slim and youthful. However appetising the food, she always claimed not to be hungry, though he suspected that she gorged on chocolates in private. Her manner remained girlish or kittenish, as if she thought that she were charming everyone, but effortful charm was, in his opinion, second only to downright rudeness in its capacity to anger.

Having once told Geoffrey that he was the universal legatee, for now, he had some pleasure in telling him that he had since been disinherited.

'At least,' he said, with a faint smile, 'for now.'

Hope must not be eradicated completely, expunged totally from the human heart; that would be cruel. But in any case, Geoffrey, like all the others in the family, was fully aware that neither inheritance nor disinheritance was final; whoever was the legatee after him would not remain in the testator's favour for long. In essence, it was a like a game of pass-the-parcel, the death of the testator being the equivalent in this case of the cessation of the music. Whoever was the universal legatee of the last will made won the prize, as it were; the question was who it would be.

Whenever he wrote anew those fateful words, 'I, being of sound mind…' he always destroyed all previous versions, and let it be known that he had done so.

Strictly speaking, neither of the women to whom he had been married, or the last woman with whom he had lived, Catherine, had any claim on the estate. They would each come to the funeral, mainly to spite the others. Divorcing from two and separating from the last, to whom he had never been married, he had drawn up legal agreements to the effect that he had fulfilled all his financial obligations to them and that the settlement was full and final. This did not mean, naturally, that he was prohibited from making any one of them his heir, and he did so from time to time, before tearing up and burning the document in which he did so.

Catherine had been his secretary once. She had been

cunning rather than intelligent, though not so cunning that he had not seen what she was up to. In a certain way she had remained his employee rather than his companion. He had also been her teacher because, when she had first come to him, she had been so ignorant, or rather had had such narrow horizons. She had never tasted wine, let alone good wine, and did not even know which knife to use in which order in a formal place setting. Becoming a secretary had been for her a rise in the social scale, having married a working-class man very early in her life, one for whom work was a regrettable expedient to be avoided if at all possible. The focus of his existence had been the pub and the football pools, and her life had been a constant struggle to protect their daughter from the consequences of his fecklessness.

Catherine had not been attracted to him only because of the better life he offered her, though that, naturally enough, had been the interpretation of his second wife, Elizabeth. But he needed no such means to attract women to him, as Elizabeth well knew, considering how many times she had accused him, with only eighty to ninety per cent accuracy, of infidelity. It was her own fault, her distress at his affairs. What business had she going through the pockets of his suits and jackets, finding billets-doux? Had she never heard that what the eye doesn't see, the heart can't grieve over? This had been the destruction of the trust that must exist for any couple to live happily together. She had even gone as far as to accuse him of leaving them there deliberately to humiliate her, 'lying about', as she called it, as if a letter folded in four and inserted in the inside pocket of a jacket could have been said to be 'lying about'. On the grounds that you might as well be hanged for a sheep as a lamb, he thenceforth did leave such evidence of his infidelity lying about for her to find. There comes a time when you are tired of concealment.

Catherine had known nothing when they started to live together, not even how to boil an egg. It was surprising, when he thought about it, how many people didn't know how to boil an egg properly. The most frequent error was overboiling. Because people were afraid that it wouldn't be cooked through, they gave it an extra minute, and then another just to make sure. They also forgot that an egg continued to cook by its intrinsic heat after it was removed from the water. They had no concept of the specific heat of an egg or its rate of cooling. They thought that, once it was removed from the water, it was a finished product. And of course, they made no allowances for the size of an egg: to them, an egg was just an egg. To boil an egg properly was a matter of judgment and experience, like hanging a man, but most people didn't understand this. Hadn't Pasteur said that chance favours the mind prepared? The trouble was that Catherine did not have a prepared mind. She was one of the majority who sleepwalked through life, following rules such as that it takes four minutes to boil an egg, or three and a half minutes, through thick and thin. (He remembered her incredulity when he told her that it would take much longer to boil an egg on the summit of Mount Everest than on the banks of the Dead Sea. When water boils, she had said, it boils.) In fact, though not surprisingly, Catherine had never learned to boil an egg, at least not reliably, so that either the white ran or the yolk solidified, however man times he told her how to do it. Soft-boiled eggs, of which he was fond, were one of the causes of friction between them.

'What does it matter?' she used to say.

What did it matter? What did anything matter! If you took that attitude to boiling an egg, was it scarcely any wonder that so much these days was second-rate, never better than good enough, that is to say ugly? No one had any pride in what he did anymore. There was no attention to detail. Badly boiled eggs were the beginning of the slippery slope.

Admittedly, Catherine had not gone to seed or let herself go until shortly before she left him after yet another quarrel over a boiled egg. Despite the fact that no one would have called her pretty, she was vain. She had been neither good- nor bad-looking; her face was as profoundly ordinary as her mind and soul had been, a face made for a crowd, as it were. What a mind it was! She read nothing, thought nothing. If he had had to describe her mind, he would have said it was like a page of a woman's magazine, consisting of fragments of unconnected trivialities. He smiled slightly at the aptness of the comparison: he might be scarcely capable of lifting his head from the pillow, but thank God his mind was as sharp as ever.

Of course, she would expect to be left something in his will: that, after all, was why she had agreed to live with him in the first place. He had been under no illusions about her feelings for him. Well, he had already given her a house as part of the separation settlement, a nasty little house it is true, but better than anything she could have hoped to own as a result of her own unaided efforts. Death would at least free him of her whining requests for assistance — financial, it went without saying — for her daughter by that feckless lout whom she had married early. This daughter, who rejoiced in the name of

Florence, was constantly undertaking courses in order to change careers, the last being in something called hair and beauty (nails probably included), though she was unattractive enough to put off any potential customer. Beautician, beautify thyself! Florence would never earn a living, at least not for more than two weeks at a time.

Catherine would probably come to the funeral if she heard of his death, because she was too stupid to realise that it would be too late for him to alter his will in her favour…

Just then, there was a knock on the door. It was the woman from the organization that distributed food to the frail elderly, including — or especially — the dying. She had a key to enter the house. She was cheerful, being from somewhere in Eastern Europe. You'd think from her manner that she was delivering a holiday feast, but the food she delivered was a sovereign remedy for appetite even for those who had any in the first place, having been cooked far away and long ago and giving off a slightly feculent smell. Moreover, it was delivered in absurd and off-putting quantities, as if designed to be thrown away — which it always was.

'Body and soul keep together!' she said, as if it were a great joke.

She left the plate just out of his reach. She was never discouraged by the fact that he never ate any of it, and always cleared away yesterday's plate to make room for today's, saying 'Tut, tut, you haven't eat nothing,' as if he were a naughty boy who had filled himself up with chocolates before mealtime. When he said that all he could manage now was a little bit of soup, she said she would tell Management, but it never made any difference. The waste of money, effort, everything, angered him: if only he had been in charge!

Yes, the country had degenerated, there could be no doubt of it. When you came to think about it, it was astonishing that it was much richer now than it was when things seemed to work properly, or at least better. No one had thrown away food in those days as they did now, and even so there was still enough left over for people to be fat. There had never been so many fat people when he was young; fat people then were very few and rich, the vests of their three-piece suits stretching over their corporations, as they were then called. Mostly they died at or about the age of sixty, a good age then.

He fell asleep as if he had actually eaten a heavy meal.

He was dreaming when he awoke with a start. He knew that his dream had been vivid and absorbing, but he could not remember its content more than a second or two after he woke. This was frustrating.

It was the nurse, or the nursing assistant, who came every day to bathe and shave him, and sometimes to change his bedclothes. She, too, was bright and cheery, a specialist in the care of the dying. She tried to make dying seem like an adventure, an old people's equivalent of what a Sunday outing used to be, except that there was no Monday to follow. But that was no cause for the dying to be downhearted.

'Let's see to you,' she said, and set to work. As she began to rub him down after removing his pyjama top, she asked 'And how are we feeling today?'

We, it was clear, were not feeling all that well. He had never been one for the emollient and meaningless social niceties, or obedience to the convention that one did not discomfit others by telling the truth rather than use the lubricating formulae of reassurance.

'How do you think I feel?' he said. His skin hung loose around his frame.

'Now, now!' she said. 'None of that negative thinking.'

That was the worst thing about dying: everyone meant well, in a professional, almost abstract, way. Good intention, he thought, what crimes are committed in thy name! Outright malice might be more supportable; at least it was sincere.

'Is there anything more I can do for you today?' she asked, having washed his face.

'As a matter of fact, there is,' he said.

She glanced at her watch.

'What is it?' she asked.

'You see that drawer over there,' he replied. He was strong enough only to indicate it with his eyes.

'Yes,' she said.

'There's a document in it that begins, 'I, being of sound mind.' I want you to bring it to me.'

'Of course.'

She brought it.

'Now tear it into little pieces, as small as you can.'

She began to do so.

'Smaller! Smaller!'

When the paper was reduced almost to confetti, he told her to throw the pieces away.

'But before you do so, I want you to bring me two pieces of blank paper and a pen.'

These tasks accomplished, the nurse, or nursing assistant, took her leave.

'See you tomorrow,' she said.

'Perhaps.'

'Now, now!'

He was about to make the supreme effort of his life. The supreme effort was to do something that, only a few months ago, he might have accomplished without awareness of effort at all: write a will.

He had a sloping bed-table on which he placed books or magazines or letters so that he could read them without sitting up. He put the paper on the bed-table and began to write.

'I, being of sound mind…'

He let fall the pen. He looked at his writing: it was spindly, shaky, as if written during an earthquake, but legible. So much the better! Let them argue over whether or not it indicated mental incapacity!

Having rested and gathered a little strength, he took up the pen again.

'hereby rescind all other wills I have made, attaching hereto a list of all that I have previously made…"

The writing of this longer passage left him breathless for a while. Though he had little to say, and both wanted and needed to be succinct, it was going all the same to be a struggle to finish; he was not even certain that he could or would manage it.

'and renounce their provisions utterly.'

This time he set down the pen with some satisfaction. At the very least, he would now die intestate, and as everyone knows, intestacy creates many problems. A smile played over his withered lips. But intestacy would not be enough to meet his purposes.

'I do this because I have long been aware of the desire to inherit that has been the sole motive of the visits to me of my relatives, both blood and by marriage.'

This had taken him several bouts of great effort, but he read the result of them with complacency. A longer rest was now necessary, and he dozed.

He woke with a start. It was urgent that he should continue.

'I therefore give and bequeath all my worldly possessions, including landed property, house, effects, monies, and all financial assets, without any restriction whatsoever to...'

Naturally, he had devoted some thought to this. In fact, he had researched it when he had still been able to do so, in the early stages of what he knew to be his last illness. What he had wanted was to find the most ridiculous and therefore humiliating legatee possible.

'the Society for the Protection of Injured Hedgehogs...'

It was almost worth dying to be able to imagine their faces when they read this, their consternation, their fury. So much money for the supposed benefit of these flea-ridden little animals that most of them had never seen except when squashed in the road by a passing car!

'and I desire that the funds be used to establish a permanent hospital for the use of the Society in its work to preserve this species that is in danger of extinction in our country.'

His instructions could hardly have been clearer. He assigned a space for his signature and that of a witness. When he finished, he had almost a song in his heart, and he sunk back in the refreshing sleep that comes after a hard, important and worthwhile task successfully accomplished.

The next day, the lady who delivered his lunch arrived as usual, that is to say at a time when nobody ate lunch. For the first time, he expressed an interest in her.

'Where are you from?' he asked.

'Albania,' she said.

'Oh, nice,' he said. 'Beautiful. Illyria.'

'My home very beautiful,' she said, surprised and delighted by this sudden regard. 'But very poor.'

'I suppose that's why you're here?'

'Yes, I build house at home.'

'That's very good. Of course, you can read and write?' he asked. 'I can tell that you're educated.'

'Yes, I read and write.'

'I knew it. I want you now to do something for me.'

He spoke quietly and with breathless pauses between words. He placed the documents on his bed-table.

'Watch me sign,' he said.

He could not complete his signature in one movement. His signature resembled a little that of Shakespeare on his deathbed, but he was satisfied that it was nevertheless his own.

'Now you sign,' he said after he had finished. 'As a witness.'

She did as she was asked. He dated the document and put it down.

'Thank you. You know the glass bowl in the dining room?'

'No, I not know the house…'

He knew that this was not true. She had an appraising eye.

'Take it,' he said. 'It is my thanks for doing this for me.'

'I will.' As she left, she said, 'Tomorrow I see you.'

'No,' he said.

He settled back and closed his eyes. His work was done: he

had sown all that he could. He would not live to see the harvest, of course, but he enjoyed the contemplation of it.

What confusion, what bitterness, what conflict, what waste of time and treasure, would he have provoked from beyond the grave! They would try to deny that he had been in his right mind and that the Albanian witness had known what she was signing. He had been careful to list the wills that he had made so that each of the persons mentioned might, and certainly would, assert a special claim as his favoured legatee. And he had chosen the Society for the Protection of Injured Hedgehogs with care, for among its trustees was a well-known, if eccentric, lawyer, who would surely fight for the Society's rights. It would take years to sort out, not counting the permanent enmities fostered between his descendants and wider family.

The next day, the woman who, for form's sake, delivered his lunch found him dead. He had died peacefully in the night. Was it a smile or a rictus on his face?

PANTHER

Although Mr Robert Smith was what used to be called a confirmed bachelor, he did not like cats. Nasty, sly creatures! They were elegant, true, but their way of slinking about so silently gave you the impression that they always had something to hide, that they were up to no good. And of course, they really did have something to hide, for they were always killing other creatures for the sake of killing them. Why did they kill birds, for example? They didn't need them for food. Moreover, cats were not even companionable. They had a lust for killing; they were born with motiveless malignity.

Dogs were not like that. Dogs were companionable. Unfortunately, Mr Smith could not have a dog because he was a schoolmaster who was away much of the time from the small flat near to the school where he taught science. It would not be fair to leave a dog in such a confined space so often, so long and for so much of its life. But Mr Smith was a sensible man: he kept his regrets within bounds and generally counted his blessings.

He was lucky that he taught at a well-established private school for the sons of the commercially successful and professional classes. To have taught in a school in which the main task of the teachers was to try to keep the insolence of the pupils — students, as they called them these days — within some kind of limits would have been a nightmare. On the other hand, to teach boys who were eager to learn was one of the greatest pleasures possible, and on the whole the boys at his school were eager, or at least willing, to learn. Of course, there was the odd bad egg, the rebel by temperament, and when a boy in his school was bad, he was very bad — drugs, crime, that sort of thing. But bad eggs were few and the school being private, they could easily be expelled without anybody having to go to the trouble of finding them an alternative. Anyway, if a child didn't want to learn, what was the point of keeping him at school? Education was not baby-sitting. A child who didn't want to learn was not merely no use to himself in school but a positive drag on the others who wanted to learn. He was disruptive, always on the lookout for distractions, not only for himself but for others, like an evangelist for inattentiveness, as if justifying his own inability to concentrate. For such a boy, twenty wrongs made a right. But really there was no need for Mr Smith to dwell on these matters, for they affected him hardly at all. However, he found a certain comfort in lamentation when what was lamented was at a distance.

Mr Smith was the least menacing of schoolteachers. He kept order not by threat or raised voice, but somehow, no doubt unconsciously, by conveying to the boys that to misbehave, as they sometimes did with teachers discovered to be weak rather than dignified, would simply be wrong, almost unthinkable. His tweed jackets with leather patches at the elbows exerted a calming effect even on the most turbulent souls. The fact is that only the kindly and well-intentioned dressed as did he.

His favourite pastime was birdwatching, the most peaceable of hobbies. He had even contributed to the ornithological literature; Notes on the Destruction of the Habitat of the Hedge-sparrow and The Decline of the Coal Tit Reconsidered had been well-received, admittedly in a restricted circle. Those who cared about such things were ever fewer, though those who did care about them cared about them more. Young people cared for the environment, but not for the birds that inhabited it; most of them couldn't tell a hawk from a handsaw.

He held his friends, or acquaintances, at arm's length; his sister lived a hundred miles away and had two children whom he thought of as 'the spoiled brats', though they were now grown up and had good jobs and children of their own. He was content enough in his isolation.

His flat was in a street of large Victorian houses that had once been occupied by a single family (and its servants) but were now divided into flats of various sizes. His bedroom on the second floor, overlooked the road through a large bay-window. The street was generally very quiet, though occasionally on Saturday nights a few drunken rowdies went by, looking for a party that they thought was being held somewhere in the street. Many of the front gardens had been asphalted over to make space for cars. The street-lighting, thank goodness, was still old-fashioned, that is to say not too bright, and cast a kind of yellowing gloom over everything rather than the brilliant glare that was now de rigueur in most of the unsleeping city.

Mr Smith had reached the age of insomnia, however. This was physiological rather than the result of a bad conscience. He had difficulty in getting off to sleep and he woke early. His lack, or rather shortness, of sleep did not leave him particularly tired, but being a man of routine, he thought there was a time to sleep and a time to wake, and unfortunately his nervous system seemed not to agree.

He had a small table by the window at which he would sit, reading, marking essays and the like, until sleep would come. One evening, just like the others, he sat there working on his latest ornithological paper, Observations on the Feeding Habits of Urban Herons. How easy it was, he thought, to take no notice of the things going on around one, as most people failed to do, taking everything for granted as if it always had been, and always would be, there. He was forever telling his pupils to look around them: that, not the cheap distractions that the modern world offered, was the way to stave off the boredom of which they so often complained and which was so often at the root of ill conduct. Did they listen to him? Mostly, not; but if he convinced one of twenty or thirty, he had more than justified both his salary and his existence.

He looked out of the window. He had come to the Methods section of his paper, in which he described the means by which he had surveyed the behaviour patterns of urban herons. His mind was still dwelling on herons when he received a visual shock. He blinked and strained forward to confirm that he had seen what he had seen.

There was now no doubt about it: he had seen what he thought he had seen. Down the centre of the road loped a panther. The reflex of its eye was caught in one of the street-lamps and flashed like a fiery jewel. It was no hallucination.

He watched it until it disappeared from view, which was not long. A panther: that was to say either a melanotic leopard or jaguar, more likely a leopard because leopards were more frequently kept in captivity, but in either case dangerous to Man. They were certainly beautiful in their way, but should not have been out walking, or stalking, our streets. It was obviously Mr Smith's duty to call the police.

At that time of night, he was put through with comparative ease, though to whom he could not tell and was not told. It was a woman, that's all he knew.

'I'm a science teacher,' he said to whomever was his interlocutor, thereby establishing his locus standi. 'I have just seen a panther on the loose walking down the street.'

'A panther, you say?'

'A melanotic, that is to say black-coated, variant of either a leopard or jaguar, Panthera pardus or Panthera onca, though I think the former is the more likely.'

'What time was this?' came the bored voice, as if panthers in the city, or reports of panthers in the city, were commonplace.

'About three or four minutes ago.'

'In what direction was it headed?'

There was obviously a checklist for panther sightings.

'It was going towards Sebastopol Road.'

'Does it answer to any name?'

'Does it answer to any name? I'm not taking about a domestic cat, but a dangerous, wild animal on the loose. You can't tame leopards or jaguars, and they can kill.'

'We haven't received any reports of a missing panther.'

In fact, people were always reporting strange things: aliens, flying saucers, crocodiles, giant snakes. There had already been a hippopotamus that evening.

'Look, I'm not imagining it,' said Mr Smith. If she had known him better, she would have appreciated that Mr Smith was a man of reality, not imagination.

'I've recorded it,' said the telephonist. 'I'll pass the message on. Thanks for your call.' The line went dead.

Mr Smith looked at the receiver accusingly, as if the incomprehension of the telephonist had been its fault. He resolved, as a responsible citizen, that he could not leave matters as they were. He would have to try again. He spoke this time to a different telephonist.

'I've just tried to report a leopard or jaguar at large in the city,' he said.

'And the name was?'

He heard the clicking of a computer keyboard.

'It's already been logged,' said the second telephonist. 'We're looking into it. Thank you for your call.' And the line went dead again.

Should he try again? Third time lucky was a foolish superstition. There was no point. Long years of pedagogy had taught him that the obtuse were incorrigible: incorrigibility was genetic in origin. He would have to wait until the morning to go to the police station in person. Night staff were usually of the lowest calibre: that is why they consented to work at night. Besides, leopards and jaguars were nocturnal creatures, so it would be dangerous to venture out.

Mr Smith had never been to a police station before, not

having had any occasion to visit one. The comings and goings of men in lumpish suits and heavy black shoes through a door with a coded lock, which was adjacent to the counter with a thick glass screen at which members of the public were received, intrigued and puzzled him. They looked so busy, purposeful and harassed, these men; but what were they doing? At the same time, they gave the impression of being disorganised and inefficient, passing in and out several times in succession, as if panicking in a crisis. There was a hieratic self-importance about them.

Suddenly the door opened, and three young men of feral expression emerged, having just been released from custody. Dressed in hooded track-suit tops, they made quickly for the entrance, as if their release might be rescinded. They were like the useless fish that fishermen throw back into the sea from their nets after pulling them on to the deck of their boat.

Mr Smith approached the counter with the thick plate glass between him and a woman seated behind it. She was intent upon what she was doing: transferring papers from her left side to her right. She didn't look up, making an heroic effort not to see Mr Smith.

'Good morning,' he said. His words seemed to bounce off the plate glass. 'Good morning,' he tried again, this time at a slightly higher volume.

The woman behind the glass didn't hear, but she must have reacted to a movement caught in the corner of her eye.

'Good morning,' said Mr Smith for a third time. Again, his words died as he uttered them. Instead of replying with words, the woman behind the counter repeatedly pointed downwards.

Mr Smith looked downwards. Perhaps (though how would she have known it?) his fly was undone or his shoelace untied. No, there was nothing untoward like that, not even a stain on his tie.

At last, the woman said something, though the sound seemed to come not directly though her mouth, but through a kind of distorting sonar fog caused by a microphone.

'Speak into the grille,' she said.

Mr Smith had to stoop uncomfortably to do so, twisting himself downwards. He said 'Good morning' for the fourth time, and heard it transmit: hardly his own voice anymore.

'Yes,' said the woman. 'How can I help you?' The offer did not sound very eager.

'I've come to report a very dangerous animal on the loose,' he said.

'You'll have to wait your turn,' she said. 'Sit over there by that lady.' She pointed to a bench against a wall on which sat a fat and blowsy woman with a black eye, who had managed to squeeze herself somehow into an extremely tight pink top and apple-green bicycle leggings. Mr Smith went and sat next to her. He had never been so close, physically, to anyone like her. His problem of whether or how to address her was solved for him.

'Hello, dear,' she said. 'What are you here for?'

He noticed that she was without teeth, which gave to her speech a slight susurrating quality. Mr Smith had often envied, if not admired or imitated, the easy familiarity with which the lower orders communicated with strangers. They seemed to love confiding in one another. He supposed it was for lack of anything else to talk about.

'I saw something very strange last night,' he said in answer to her question.

'Yes,' she said. 'I don't know what the world's coming to. See this?' She pointed to her black eye. 'This time, he's gone too far. I've had just about enough of him.'

'Who?'

'Him indoors.' She gestured with her head as if he were just around the corner. 'I'm not putting up with it no more.'

Apparently, he had come home drunk, picked a quarrel, hit her, removed her false teeth from the glass by the bed in which she had placed them, and stamped on them until they were unrecognisable.

'And they was the best pair I ever had,' she said, as if this added to the heinousness of his conduct.

Mr Smith hadn't known there were people in the world like this. He almost forgot about the leopard or jaguar (probably a leopard) as she related her story. Like a fool, she said, she had believed him last time when he said he was sorry and would never do it again, that he would change.

'A leopard never changes its spots,' she said.

This time, she really thought that he was going to kill her, he had such a look in his eyes, as if he didn't really know what he was doing, as if he had lost all control. Well, this time she was going to see it through if it killed her — she meant the court case. This time he wasn't going to get away with it like he always had before. She'd always known he was no good. People had warned her when she first got together with him. Don't touch him with a bargepole, they'd said, and they were right, but she'd thought he would change for her, only he never...

'Next!' shouted the woman behind the counter into her microphone, as if she had already been dealing with a long procession of people.

The woman with the black eye waddled over to the counter. Evidently it was not her first time: she was familiar with the procedure. The woman behind the counter was familiar with her, too.

'Here again, Rose?' she said. 'Same as usual?'

'Worse this time,' said Rose. 'He never done my teeth before. It'll be months before I can get a new set.'

'You're not going to drop the charges again this time, are you?'

'No, this time I'm going through with it.'

'You know the inspector said that at some point you would have to be charged with wasting police time.'

Rose was indignant.

'It's not my fault he's like this.'

The woman behind the counter took the details and entered them in a computer. When she had finished, she told Rose to go over to another bench, that of processed complainants, and to wait there. Rose went obediently. After all, much of her life had been spent waiting; waiting for a beating, waiting her turn, waiting for her pension or social security payment. Waiting was her profession, her pastime and her fate.

The woman behind the counter appeared to be in no hurry. She was expert in finding little things to do that were more important than dealing with the public. Eventually, however, there was nothing for it but to do so. 'Next!' she called, and Mr Smith went over to the counter.

'Good morning,' he said yet again.

'Yes?' she said suspiciously. She had lost the bantering tone she had adopted with Rose. With Rose, you knew where you were: nothing would come of it. But with someone new, it was possible that some action would be required.

'I've come to report a dangerous wild animal that I saw last night, a leopard or a jaguar, the black melanotic variety, probably a leopard, walking down the road. I couldn't sleep last night and saw it out of my window.'

'Name?' 'Oh yes, of course. Robert Smith.' 'Address?' 'Age?' 'Date of birth?' 'Married, single, divorced or widowed?'

The essentials recorded, the woman said, 'So you say you saw a dangerous animal. How do you know it was dangerous?'

'Because leopards or jaguars are dangerous. In fact, they are some of the few predators that will kill just for the pleasure of it — unlike lions, for example.' Mr Smith could never resist the temptation to tell people things they did not know; he was a confirmed pedagogue.

The woman behind the counter rested her head on her fist, her elbow resting on the arm of her chair. It was obvious that she thought that she was dealing with some kind of madman.

'How do you know it was a leopard?'

'A leopard or a jaguar,' corrected Mr Smith. 'They are the only two Felidae with a melanotic, that is to say black, genetic variant. I studied zoology for two years at university.'

'You might have been mistaken, seeing a moving shadow for example.'

'I might,' said Mr Smith. As a scientist, he had always to admit the possibility of error. 'But I don't think so.'

'Had you been drinking?'

Had he been drinking? What a question! As a schoolmaster, however, he was used to, and knew how to deal calmly with, impertinence.

'No,' he replied. 'I'm a schoolteacher and I had classes the following morning.'

The woman behind the counter gave him an appraising look. Those in denial were always the worst.

'We've had seven sightings of Lord Lucan this year,' she said, 'to say nothing of flying saucers. That's why I'm asking.'

'This is different…'

'We've had no other reports. Still, I'll pass it on.'

'I think it's urgent. Someone… someone…' He was going to say that someone might be killed, but the woman behind the counter had switched off the microphone with an audible click, and again his words fell dead as he uttered them. She resumed the important task of sorting her papers.

Mr Smith returned home feeling defeated. What should he do now? There were none so deaf as would not hear, yet it was his bounden duty as a citizen to warn people of the danger. He who had always lived quietly, anonymously, must now step forward. They must, at the very least, be told to be on the lookout, alert to the possibilities. Leopards were partial to dogs, which should therefore be kept at home, especially at night, when they should not be walked. Small children in particular were vulnerable, for however powerful a predator might be, it always preferred an easy prey to one that might struggle. And though the Felidae were nocturnal, that did not mean that there was no danger at all by day. If disturbed during sleep, they would immediately turn vicious.

Mr Smith realised when he returned home that he had

missed his first class of the day. He had never done such a thing before, nor even had a day's illness. In fact, he had been a man by whom, like Kant, people might have set their watches! Strange how he had forgotten about his first class of the day, then. Now he would have to explain his totally unaccustomed non-appearance. He decided that truth, like honesty, would be the best policy, but only for the ears of the highest authority, the headmaster. When he telephoned the school, therefore, he asked to be put through to him.

Mr Smith regretted the loss of his colleagues' habit of calling each other by their surnames. Somehow first-name terms seemed to imply a false sense of intimacy. In his earlier days, such first-name terms had been reserved for very few, if any at all. It was the headmaster, now in post for twenty years, who had insisted on the change as part of what he called modernisation. He wasn't really a bad chap, the headmaster, but a little given to innovation for its own sake.

'It's Smith here,' he said when finally put through. 'Robert.'

'Ah Robert,' said the headmaster. 'We were wondering what'd happened to you.'

News of his absence had reached the head, then: of course it had. It would have been he who had to decide what to do about the class with an unexpectedly absent teacher. In fact, it had been he who had stepped into the breach.

'I had to go to the police, headmaster,' said Mr Smith.

'The police? Whatever for?' Robert and the police were impossible to imagine in the same sentence.

'I had to report something. It was my duty.'

'What was it, Robert?'

Even after all these years, to be addressed by the

headmaster as Robert gave him a little shock, as if he had been connected by wires to a battery of small voltage. Interestingly, the headmaster never insisted on being addressed by his first name.

'Last night I witnessed something very alarming,' he said. 'I was sitting at my window — I couldn't sleep — and I saw a large cat walk by, a member of the Felidae, either a leopard or a jaguar, of a melanotic variation. Probably a leopard.'

There was a silence at the other end of the phone. The silence seemed to have a positive quality — a meaning — rather than being a mere absence of sound.

'I tried to report it to the police by telephone,' Mr Smith — Robert — continued. 'I called them twice. They obviously didn't believe me, so I felt it necessary to report it in person this morning at the station. I would have gone to the station last night but... well, with such an animal about...'

The silence from the other end persisted. He felt obliged to say something more, to elaborate.

'The Felidae are nocturnal,' he said. The headmaster was a classicist and couldn't be expected to know that. In fact, secretly, his view of education was rather narrow. He thought that only people like himself were truly educated.

'I realise that I should have called earlier, but I was so alarmed that I didn't think of it. I'm sorry, headmaster, I apologise. It won't happen again.'

The silence continuing, Mr Smith wondered whether, perhaps, they had been cut off. The telephone these days was much more reliable than formerly, but nevertheless there were still sometimes irregularities in its operation.

'Are you still there, headmaster?' he asked.

'Yes, Robert, I'm listening.'

'Yes, well, I have a fifth form at eleven o'clock. I should be able to make it if I leave straight away.'

'I think I should take the day off if I were you,' said the headmaster. 'After last night, perhaps you need a rest.'

'No, I'm perfectly all right, really I am, headmaster. I'll be at school in a few minutes.'

'Well, before you go to the class, perhaps you would be so good as to call at my office first.'

'Of course, headmaster.'

Mr Smith, naturally, was good as his word. He arrived at the outer sanctum of the headmaster's office (it would once have been called his study), over which Miss Forster presided as militarily as any praetorian guard.

'The Head wanted to see me,' said Mr Smith.

Miss Forster, officious as ever, spoke at once, but not altogether approvingly, over the interphone to the headmaster.

'Yes, Miss Forster,' he said when the buzzer sounded. He did not insist with her on the familiarity of first name terms.

'Mr Smith is here to see you, Headmaster,' she said.

'Just ask him to wait for a moment, could you, Miss Forster.'

Although Mr Smith must have heard the message perfectly well, Miss Forster relayed it to him herself.

'Ask Mr Smith to come in,' said the head after a delay just long enough to increase Mr Smith's anxiety.

'Come in, Robert, come in,' said the headmaster, rising from behind his desk. 'Sit down. Make yourself comfortable.'

'Thank you, Headmaster,' said Mr Smith. 'Good of you to see me.' He realised at once that it was a foolish thing to have said. After all, it was the headmaster who had asked to see him. His words sounded almost like an admission of guilt. How humiliating to have reached his age and yet still be as nervous as a small boy!

'How are you, Robert?' asked the headmaster.

Mr Smith disliked solicitude, especially when it was purely formal. The real variety embarrassed him, the formal irritated him. 'You must be tired after your adventure last night?'

'Not at all, Headmaster.' He noted the word adventure, with its slight tone of ironic disparagement, but said nothing.

'What did the police say?'

'To be frank, Headmaster, they seemed not to be very interested, casual I would say. They don't seem to realise the danger such animals pose. I suppose that the only cats they know are the kind that get stuck up trees.'

'I think that's the Fire Brigade, Robert,' said the headmaster.

'Quite so, Headmaster. At any rate, I did my duty.'

'Naturally.'

'I've done all I can, and so now I'm returning to my school duties.'

The headmaster rubbed his chin like a magician conjuring a genie from a bottle, the genie in this case being a thought. Eventually, he said, 'You haven't shaved today, Robert.'

Mr Smith rubbed his chin in turn.

'That's true, Headmaster. I went to the police as soon as I woke this morning and hadn't time before coming to school.'

'We have standards to keep up, Robert.'

'Of course, Headmaster.'

He was himself a man who believed in standards, in fact he

insisted on them, but he thought nevertheless that it was a little pedantic of the headmaster, a little lacking in imagination, to draw attention to the matter in these circumstances — the first time in decades, moreover.

'Forgive me for saying so, Robert, but you look a little dishevelled.'

'I had to dress very quickly this morning, Headmaster. I hadn't time even to look at myself in the glass.'

'Pity,' said the headmaster. After a pause, he resumed. 'Here's what I think. I think you should go home now. You need a rest. You've probably been working too hard recently — all the added administration these days.'

So that was it! The headmaster thought that he was imagining it all, making it up, hallucinating. In short, that he was mad.

'I'd like you to see someone,' said the headmaster. 'For your health. I could make an appointment for you.'

'Really, I feel perfectly well, Headmaster.'

'Louis told me two or three weeks ago that he thought you were beginning to feel the strain.'

Louis was Louis Lingard, the new young science teacher who was ambitious and from the first had wanted to take over from Mr Smith as head of department. He tried to curry favour with the boys by his informal manner and habit of making jokes, but one day he would learn the error of his ways. Of course, his relaxed manner was a pose, ambition having many guises. Though he was not usually critical of his colleagues, Mr Smith had not taken to Louis Lingard.

'I don't know what could have given him that impression, Headmaster,' said Mr Smith.

'Anyhow,' said the headmaster, 'that is my decision. Occupational Health will ring you with an appointment.'

'Who will take the Fifth Form today?" asked Mr Smith. He was a devoted teacher.

'Don't worry about that, Robert. We'll take care of that.'

'When will you want me to return to duty?'

'As soon as possible, of course, Robert. But we'll have to be guided by Occupational Health.'

There was nothing for it but to return home. What else could he do? He tried to settle down to read a new book on the ecology of owls, including their population dynamics, but found that he could not concentrate. In fact, he couldn't even fix his mind properly on his situation. It was as much as he could do to follow the sequential steps in making a cup of tea.

The doorbell rang. Mr Smith spoke on his own interphone.

'Police,' came the reply.

'Police?'

'Are you Mr Robert Smith?'

'Yes.'

'You need to have a word with us.'

Was it not the other way round?

'Come in.'

At last, they were taking some action, he thought. About time.

He heard the heavy tread of two people on the stair and opened the door to his flat.

The representatives of the police force entered, a man and a woman. They both wore stab-vests. That of the man, who was pudgy and slightly breathless from the exertion of climbing the stairs, left a little of his stomach exposed above the waist, his black shirt showing. From their wide belts, like ornaments on a Christmas tree, were festooned the apparatus of repression, such as handcuffs, gas cannisters, and the like. They entered the flat sideways.

'You've come about my sighting of the panther?' said Mr Smith.

The two of them looked at one another, as if deciding which of them should speak.

'In a way,' said the policeman.

'Has it been recaptured?'

'Not exactly.'

'Been spotted again, then?'

'Not that either.'

'What then?'

The policewoman referred to the screen of a small electronic device that she held in her hand.

'You telephoned the station last night to report that you'd seen a panther walking down the road. The telephonist told you that we would look into it, is that correct?'

'Yes, that is correct.'

'You telephoned again immediately afterwards, is that correct?'

'Yes.'

'And you were again told that we would look into it, is that correct?'

'Yes.'

'And this morning at eight o'clock, you reported it again in person at the station, is that correct?

'Yes.'

'And you were told a third time that we would look into

it?'

'Yes. Have you found anything — you the police, I mean?'

The policeman took over from the woman.

'We haven't come about that,' he said.

'About what, then?'

'We've come to warn you not to waste police time.'

'I haven't wasted any police time,' said Mr Smith in as near to a tone of protest as he ever came.

'That's not for you to say.'

'We've come here,' said the policewoman, 'to tell you that if you persist in nuisance reporting, you will be charged.'

'I'm a trained scientist,' said Mr Smith, 'trained to observe accurately. I don't go around imagining things. I saw what I saw, and what I saw was a panther...'

'We're warning you,' said the policeman. 'I wouldn't say anything more if I was you.'

'We've got a paper for you to sign,' interjected the policewoman. 'It's to say that you acknowledge that you've received this warning.' She produced a paper. It said that he, Robert Smith, thereby acknowledged that if he repeated his reports, he would be subject to prosecution, and that he undertook not to spread public alarm by such report.

'I haven't spread any public alarm.'

'You told the headmaster,' said the policeman. 'And the children are vulnerable.'

So the police had been investigating him, not the panther! They had time for that, but not time for...

'Are you going to sign?' asked the policeman. 'We haven't got all day.'

'And what if I don't?'

'The sergeant'll have decide what to do. It's not up to us. But he says he's getting fed up with all these reports he's been having, wasting our time.'

The policewoman interjected again.

'Why don't you just sign? You've got nothing to lose.'

'Since we're not going to make any more false reports, are we?' said her colleague, with a slightly twisted mouth.

'I'll think about it,' said Mr Smith.

'It's too late for that,' said the policeman. 'We're not coming again. It's time for yes or no.'

Mr Smith was not an impulsive man, but he took the paper, flattened it on the table and signed. Though he was innocent, it felt like an admission of guilt. The policeman and policewoman clattered clumsily down the stairs with a sense of accomplishment, of a job done.

Mr Smith had now to await his appointment with Occupational Health. It came by telephone, three days later. The woman who telephoned him told him he was lucky, there had been a cancellation. That's why the appointment was at such short notice.

The building in which Dr Freesland received him was not such as Mr Smith would have imagined to house a medical facility. It was more like an office block than a hospital. Indeed, on the panel listing all the occupants of the building were an accountant, a public relations company, an employment agency and a company called Small Solutions, though it did not say to what.

Dr Freesland was a quiet, grey, defeated man, who had the air of an office worker just before a not very prosperous retirement. He asked Mr Smith to sit down opposite him at his desk. He asked a long series of banal questions about how Mr Smith was eating, sleeping and generally getting on with life. He attended mostly to his computer screen, but from time to time glanced furtively at Mr Smith, as if trying to catch him out in something. Then he said, 'I've heard you had an unusual experience lately?'

'Yes,' said Mr Smith, and described what he had seen.

'Have you seen it again lately?'

As it happened, Mr Smith had looked out of his window the night before and thought he had seen something, a moving shadow that could have been the panther, though he wasn't sure.

Dr Freesland expressed no surprise, or anything else. It was as if, at the end of his career, nothing anyone said could have any interest for him. Then he walked round his desk to where Mr Smith was sitting and took his blood pressure, just to prove, perhaps, that he was a doctor.

A few days later, Mr Smith had a telephone call from the headmaster.

'I've had Dr Freesland's report,' he said. 'I'm afraid he makes it quite clear that he thinks you should be retired on medical grounds.'

'But I feel perfectly well, Headmaster.'

'He is categorical that we can't take the risk. Our insurance wouldn't cover us. It's really out of my hands, Robert. I'm sorry about that.'

A few days later in the press and on television, there was excitement about a melanotic jaguar that had been shot dead by the police about a mile from Mr Smith's flat. Apparently, it had been brought into the country by a notorious drug-dealer and had escaped from the grounds of his mansion in the vicinity.

In a fever of triumphant vindication, Mr Smith telephoned the headmaster. Getting through was not easy, however: he had to be persistent.

'So you see, Headmaster,' he said, 'I wasn't imagining it.'

'I never said that you were, Robert.'

True, he had never actually said it, but clearly he had thought it. And seeing things was a sign of madness.

'When can I start back at work, Headmaster?'

There was a pause.

'I'll have to clear it with Dr Freesland first,' said the headmaster.

'How long will that take?' asked Mr Smith.

'Not long, I should imagine'

A few days later, Miss Forster called him.

'Are you free to speak to the Headmaster?'

Free? What else might he have been doing?

'I've spoken to Dr Freesland,' said the headmaster. 'He can't see any reason to change his opinion.'

HILDA AND SAMUEL

When marriages are bad, they are an inexhaustible source of misery; when they are good, they are an enduring source of happiness. Hilda and Samuel's marriage could not have been better.

They had been married for fifty years. Not only had no one ever heard a cross word ever pass between them, but not one who knew them could even imagine such a word had ever passed between them. Their benignity was general, as strong towards the world as to each other. They lacked the hard edge of saintliness, they disconcerted no one, their manner was unselfconscious, they were not trying to set an example or illustrate a theory, and if people who knew them ever discussed marriage, theirs was taken as a model to aspire to. Their goodness was untainted by censoriousness. They found the imperfections of humanity amusing rather than distressing: they were not disappointed by them because they expected and accepted them. As for more serious wrongdoing, they were only mildly shocked by it. Their strongest word of disapprobation for a fellow-being was 'rascal' for a man and 'gossip' for a woman. Even Hitler had only been 'a scoundrel'.

They lived in a village that had once been pretty. Its centre was still pretty, but you had only to turn a corner or walk a couple of hundred yards to come across newer houses and other buildings that were a scar on the landscape, to which no passage of time would ever lend a charm. Samuel and Hilda's cottage was ancient, full of nooks and crannies, surprisingly large in total, though no part of it gave any impression of size. It was filled with antiques for use rather than ornament and also with comfortable chintz chairs. The tick of the long-case clock seemed somehow to symbolise the calm and even tenor of their life together.

The garden was all of a piece with the house. A paved stone path led from a wooden gate up a slight incline between an avenue of old apple trees to the front door. The lawn and flowerbeds were disposed according to no geometric pattern but not merely haphazardly either, with every plant or flower setting others off in a profusion in which nothing predominated or overwhelmed. Only in the small kitchen garden were the plants regimented, but without the order for its own sake that some obsessional gardeners insist upon.

When, to the fury of the existing villagers (whose protests to the authorities had, of course, been futile) the new houses were built, Samuel and Hilda had merely said, 'Well, people have to live somewhere.'

They had had no children, though whether this was a sadness or disappointment for them no one ever knew. If anyone asked them why they had no children, they just said that it was just one of those things, they were not able to, and in those days you accepted it because there was nothing to be done in any case. Samuel and Hilda had found that

68

acceptance was the better part of contentment.

They were fond of children, however, and children were fond of them. Benignity attracts children. Hilda had been an only child herself, but Samuel had had two brothers, both deceased. Each of them had had a son, and both sons had had two children, so that Samuel and Hilda had two nephews and four great-nephews and nieces. All of them visited Hilda and Samuel quite often, three or four times a year.

The children loved their visits to their great uncle and aunt. In the summer, there being room, they would stay for a few days. It was a paradise for them. There was a pond in the garden with frogs and newts, and children are fascinated by amphibians. The newts were comparatively few, which added to the excitement of catching them, especially at the time of year when some of them had bright orange bellies. In spring, there were tadpoles to take home and grow into tiny frogs, none of which probably survived in their suburban gardens (at least, their mothers hoped not). If they took frogspawn home, it never developed very far and before long had to be thrown away, but failure never dampened their enthusiasm for it.

Before, regretfully, they left for home, Great Uncle Samuel and Great Aunt Hilda gave them presents: little toys, bags of toffees with coins (this was in the days when you could still buy things with coins). The presents made up for the return to boring normal life; and it was just possible that the expectation of the presents added to their joy at arrival in the first place.

Strangely enough for someone so benign, Samuel had been, in his earlier days, a success in business. He had inherited a grocery from his father and had built it up into a small chain, which he then sold to a much larger chain. His expansion had required only efficiency, not ruthlessness, and a willingness to adopt new methods and adapt to new tastes. He had always acted decently towards his customers, staff and suppliers. The business had provided the couple with a good living while he owned it and a very comfortable and long retirement when he sold it. Samuel and Hilda were then able to indulge their natural inclination to benevolence.

The two nephews were aware that Samuel and Hilda had a small fortune to leave and no one to leave it to. This is not to say that they did not love or admire their uncle and aunt — it was impossible not to love them. But it would not have been in accordance with human nature if the possibility of an inheritance had not existed at the back of their minds and encouraged them to maintain closer contact than might have been the case otherwise. They made especially sure that their children wrote to thank their great uncle and great aunt after their visits. This was only polite, of course, but it was not only polite. They made sure, however, that their children did not know what else it was, besides being polite.

Though the two brothers, Samuel and Hilda's nephews, were by no means enemies, they kept a wary eye on each other as far as their relations with the uncle and aunt were concerned. They hardly admitted it to themselves, but each did not want the other to advance too deeply into the old couple's affections. At the same time, they did not want them to think that they were currying favour with them. It was a delicate balancing act.

They did not keep abreast of each other's movements by direct communication but rather by speaking to their aunt and uncle by telephone. Perhaps they were not fully aware that this was what they were doing; after all, Hilda and Samuel were advancing in years and it was only right that they should not be abandoned to loneliness. Despite their benignity and friendliness, they did not have a wide circle of friends, though all their human relations were cordial. Samuel had had no time to make friends while he ran his business, and the time for making friends was over once he retired. And when beneficence is too general, it is difficult to show anyone that special mark of favour that is essential to friendship. Perhaps friendship requires the possibility of its opposite, of enmity.

But Samuel and Hilda were popular locally. They neither gossiped nor were the subject of gossip: for gossip is always tinged with malice and pleasure at the misfortune (or worse) of others. The fact was that no one could think of anything malicious to say about them, and even to have tried to do so would have been a breach of village etiquette. Samuel and Hilda gave generously to the church and supported its restoration appeal, but they attended only intermittently, such that they were regulars but without a damaging reputation for piety. Samuel drank but only a couple of glasses a day; they had a cat and a dog, who naturally got on very well together, and the dog did not bother the sheep in the nearby fields, as several other local dogs did.

As time passed, their great nieces and nephews ceased to be interested in frogs and newts: indeed, soon after they lost interest, they could hardly remember why they had been so fascinated by them and looked back with embarrassment on their earlier enthusiasm, as being a guilty mark of childishness. Their parents, however, insisted that they continue to visit the old couple, although they were now nearly grown up and none of their friends visited their uncles and aunts, let alone their great-uncles and aunts. Such obligatory visits now seemed to them a measure of immaturity: they were almost ashamed of them, and they were no longer as financially rewarding as they had been, not because Samuel and Hilda gave them less, but because their needs (or desires) had increased.

'Why do we have to go?' they would ask before every projected visit. They had reached the age at which they wanted to do only what they wanted to do and already had secret desires. 'Why can't they come to us instead?'

'Hilda and Samuel are on their own. They've got no one else.'

'I still can't see why they don't come to us instead. They've never come to us.'

'Uncle Samuel doesn't like to drive, and Aunt Hilda doesn't know how. She doesn't like going in the car anyway.'

Sometimes the answer was different.

'Your cousins went last week.'

'So what? Why does that mean that we have to go?'

'You wouldn't want Uncle Samuel and Aunt Hilda to think they were better than you.'

They wouldn't have minded that at all, because what Samuel and Hilda thought of them was no longer of great interest to them. Of course, they still liked them — it was impossible not to — but there is a difference between liking people and wanting to spend time with them.

Despite having been told that Hilda and Samuel did not like to travel, one day one of the children, James, overheard his parents discussing a possible visit by them.

'It's going to be awkward. Where are we going to put them?'

'In the spare bedroom, of course.'

'We couldn't do that. It wouldn't be right. It would be disgusting.'

'Oh come on, don't be so narrow-minded.'

'I'm not being narrow-minded. How would you like it if…?'

'I don't think we have to worry about that. It's never going to happen. After all, Hilda and Samuel are…'

'It's a matter of principle.'

'It's been going on forever. It wouldn't change anything if they came here. It's far too late for that.'

'But that's not the point. It would be in our house…'

'You have to think of the children's future. If Hilda and Samuel thought that we were being hostile just because…'

'Surely we can find some excuse to put them off. We don't have to let them know why…'

'They're not stupid. They'd guess. It's the first time they've ever asked to come, and we'd have refused.'

'We'll have to find a reason. It shouldn't be that difficult.'

This conversation seemed to James like a series of clues to a crossword puzzle. Whatever it meant, Samuel and Hilda didn't ever come to stay.

Hilda fell ill, and like many people who have gone through life without a day's illness, she deteriorated rapidly, as if she lacked practice in being ill. It was cancer, they said, though they never found where it had started. That was why it spread so rapidly: they didn't know what to cut out.

They all went to see her, of course, first at home and then in hospital. She seemed to reduce to the size of a small bird, hardly capable of fluttering. But she retained the sweetness of temper that had been hers throughout life, and she did not

73

complain. When visitors came, she was more concerned for their comfort than for her own. Samuel, who was by her side all the time, made heroic efforts not to be wretched. But his cheerfulness deceived no one.

Hilda died as peacefully as she had lived. Samuel, being of an older generation, felt it his duty not to express in public the grief that he felt, though the latter must have been fathomless. As for others, such formulaic expressions as 'Deeply regretted' and 'Sadly missed' were, for once, true.

Life lost its savour for Samuel, who had seemed previously to enjoy it so much, albeit in a quiet and undemonstrative way. Everyone considered it almost a mercy when, three months after Hilda's death, he died in his sleep, being found in his bed one morning by the cleaning lady. No one failed to say that this was how he or she would like to die: Samuel's was the best of all possible deaths.

There was a short period of tension for the two nephews before the content of Uncle Samuel's will was known. Each was certain that, secretly, he had been Uncle Samuel's favourite, but the will was completely even-handed: the very substantial estate, larger even than hoped for or expected, was divided with absolute equality between the two branches of the family, with none of the children forgotten.

A few years later, James, now a young adult, returned to his parents' conversation that he had overheard.

'Hilda and Samuel were so sweet,' he said.

'Yes, never a cross word between them, not in all their years together. Everyone loved them.'

'Then why did you not want them to come to stay?'

'Oh, they didn't like to travel.'

'But they wanted to come. I overheard you say that it would be very awkward if they did. Why was that?'

'Well, the fact is,' said James' father, obviously with some reluctance, 'that your Great-Aunt Hilda and your Great-Uncle Samuel were never really married. In fact, they weren't husband and wife. They were brother and sister, actually.'

A Cupboard under the Stairs

Number 17, Frampton Road, was, like numbers 15 and 19, and indeed all the other houses in the street, a substantial early Victorian house, its number painted in black on one of its portico's Ionic pillars. The road was named for the entrepreneur who had built it, Obadiah Frampton, and who had once lived there himself. The houses were built for the families of the prosperous commercial classes and their servants but had long since been divided into flats and even, in the less well-maintained of them, single rooms with shared bathrooms.

Number 17, however, was divided into five flats, each occupying a floor. The basement flat was occupied by Mr and Mrs Hashemi and their son, Hasheem, a fat and over-indulged little boy given to successful tantrums whenever temporarily denied whatever he wanted, which was rarely. Mr Hashemi's hours were long and irregular, for he owned a Persian restaurant three or four streets away, patronised largely by the Persian diaspora. Its food, therefore, had to be authentic.

The basement flat was quite large but somewhat gloomy.

From its narrow front windows below the level of the street outside, and between the steel bars to deter burglars, could be seen the feet of pedestrians as they walked by. You could tell quite a lot about people by their footwear, though perhaps not quite as much as from their faces; but Mr Hashemi was not interested in the niceties of such observations, as he had more than enough contact with human nature in the course of his business activities, between the lazy and dishonest staff and the fussy and demanding customers.

Mr Hashemi was not a happy man and was given to impotent querulousness. Above him, in the ground-floor flat, dwelled Mr and Mrs Khorasami, also Iranian refugees or migrants. The common national origins of the Hashemis and Khorasamis did not conduce to sympathy between them, rather the reverse. Whether their lack of mutual sympathy arose from some difference of political opinion (for exiles are inclined to be intolerant of the slightest divergencies of opinion about the situation in their country of origin), or from some other source, no outsider could tell; but Mr Khorasami obviously thought that he was a cut above Mr Hashemi. They hardly spoke except to complain about noise emanating from each other's flat.

Mr Khorasami was 'in carpets', and carpets, unlike Persian food, were art. Moreover, he had been to university, which Mr Hashemi had not. His English was better than Mr Hashemi's, and he therefore insisted that Mr Hashemi address him in that language, thus putting him immediately at a disadvantage. He would not reply if Mr Hashemi spoke to him in Farsi.

The main causes of their disputes were three: noise, as

mentioned above, parking spaces and the cupboard under the stairs in the entrance hall. Mr Hashemi, who always returned from work in a state of nervous exhaustion combined with exasperation, was hypersensitive to all noise except that which he made himself. To look at him, one would not have expected him to be sensitive to anything: he was fat and rotund, often unshaven, and seemed to exude oil like a fried aubergine squeezed with a wooden spoon. Long but few strands of bluish-black hair were plastered down over his bald pate, fooling himself when he looked in the glass but no one else.

The slightest noise from above drove him to fury. The Khorasamis were by no means noisy, but Mr Hashemi appeared to expect them to remain forever rooted to one spot and never to move across their own rooms, to drop anything or to vacuum their own carpets. If they did any of those things, Mr Hashemi was ready. With surprising agility, he would jump up and bang the ceiling with the extension of a vacuum cleaner kept expressly for that purpose. He would shout an imprecation and upstairs, as he called it, would go silent for a time. But then there would be another noise which Mr Hashemi, being of somewhat paranoid disposition, believed was directed at him.

The parking problem was the second most potent reason for Mr Hashemi's grievance against his neighbour. Mr Khorasami's Mercedes was large and new, and he kept it gleaming. Mr Hashemi's, by contrast, was second-hand and now clearly past its best. When Mr Khorasami took a parking space directly in front of Number 17, which he was perfectly entitled to do, Mr Hashemi saw red. He didn't mind if anyone else parked there, but if his compatriot and fellow part-owner of the building did so, he was reduced to a state of fury. He took it as a provocation, an insult thrown in his face. Mr Khorasami was deliberately showing off, rubbing his comparative success in Mr Hashemi's face, for the car, or at least the lower part of it, could be seen from the basement flat's windows. Whenever he caught sight of Mr Khorasami manoeuvring his car into the space, he rushed out and expostulated with him, claiming that he had been just about to move his own car into that space, and Mr Khorasami knew it. He had previously told Mr Khorasami that he had things that he needed to load into, or unload from, his car, and now he was creating difficulties for him. But Mr Khorasami responded haughtily, as if this argument was beneath his notice, and said that, as the holder of a parking permit, he was entitled to park there and the law was on his side — though Mr Hashemi suspected, on general grounds rather than from any specific evidence, that Mr Khorasami's business practices were not in total accordance with the law. His own certainly were not.

Mr Hashemi replied in his turn that he was not speaking of the law but of something more important, something apparently unknown to Mr Khorasami: good neighbourliness. His appeal, of course, would fall on deaf ears; he knew that in advance, but he uttered it only to justify the righteous indignation that he felt.

But by far the most important cause of conflict between them was the cupboard under the stairs, of which Mr Khorasami had taken de facto possession. He had been the first to buy a flat from the developer who had transformed the house into supposedly 'luxury' flats from their previous condition as sordid lodgings and had straightaway filled the cupboard with such of his belongings as he did not want to clutter his flat with. Though there was nothing valuable among them, he insisted upon placing a padlock on the door, as if they might otherwise be stolen by the other residents of Number 17.

Strictly speaking — and in this respect, Mr Hashemi spoke strictly — the cupboard belonged to all the residents in equal share, as being of what the deeds to the property called 'common parts'. They, the residents, had therefore the right to use it, though if divided into equal parts it would have been as good as useless to each and all. But that was beside the point, said Mr Hashemi: it was a matter of principle. Mr Hashemi claimed to have been a political prisoner and tortured in his native land (though most people had difficulty believing it, such were his physique and manner), and he said that he was not going to have fled Shah's tyranny only to become the subject of Mr Khorasami's — who, he said, had enjoyed a gilded youth under the reign of the Shah.

It was vital, then, that the cupboard be restored to general use, though it had never had such a use. Not only did everyone possess things that he or she would like to have kept but not to display, but the cupboard, apart from its small size, was perfectly adapted to this purpose. More important, though, was the principle of equity, if Mr Hashemi could but have named it. It did not matter to him whether anybody else actually wanted the use of the cupboard: even if no one did, the struggle against Mr Khorasami for justice would still be worthwhile. Man does not live by storage space alone.

There were five owners of Number 17, Frampton Road, each with an equal vote with regard to the common parts and all other matters affecting the whole building. Voting was by majority and, in theory, majority decisions were binding on the minority. It was Mr Hashemi's ambition to build a coalition to force Mr Khorasami to relinquish what he called his 'illegal occupation' of the cupboard.

However, such a coalition was far from easy to build. One problem was that Dan Frisk, the owner of the flat directly above Mr Khorasami's, was very seldom in occupation, and on the few and fleeting occasions when he was, he did not want to preoccupy himself with the affairs of the whole house. He was, in fact, a war photographer, and had become so used to armed conflict that anything less than war seemed to him boring and trivial: he was always longing to get back to where he might be shot at. On the rare occasions on which Mr Hashemi was able to catch him and talk to him about the affairs of Number 17, he always replied with an air of complete unconcern, saying merely 'I'm happy to go along with what all the others want.'

Mr Hashemi didn't really like Dan Frisk but was obliged to conceal it for the sake of his wider goal. One day, perhaps, Dan Frisk would be forced — by a landmine injury, for example — to live at home, and then he might be incorporated into the coalition. There was a further difficulty with Dan Frisk, though: whenever he was at home, he insisted upon leaving his elaborate and technologically advanced bicycle in the hallway, which irritated Mr Hashemi, though with what for him was superhuman effort he did not show it. This bicycle was not the simple contraption of the kind Mr

81

Hashemi had known in his impoverished childhood (impoverished in retrospect, not experienced as such at the time), and he could not see why Dan Frisk needed so expensive a model, both feather-light and extremely strong, and festooned with all kinds of extras and appurtenances. After all, he only rode it in the streets of London on rare occasions; what business had he, then, with a bicycle that must have cost thousands? Furthermore, whenever he wasn't at war, insinuating himself into trenches and field hospitals, he obviously considered himself a morally superior ecologist, reprehending the use of cars, even of Mercedes.

Why couldn't he keep his damned bicycle in his flat? It wouldn't clutter it if he did, and in any case, he was not the kind of man to notice. Mr Hashemi happened to know that his flat was untidy and disorganised precisely as you would expect from a man of his type, so the bicycle would make no difference. It was obvious to Mr Hashemi that Dan Frisk was taunting him with his bicycle, because he knew that Mr Hashemi, wanting to incorporate him into the anti-Khorasami coalition, could say nothing about it. If he wasn't an ally, at least he didn't want him as an enemy.

For the moment, then, there was no question of Dan Frisk's vote to evict Mr Khorasami from the cupboard. That left the two others, both of whom he would have to win to his side. A voting majority of five is three, but so it is of four if there is no arrangement for a chairman's casting a vote, which there was not according to Number 17's statutes. When they had been drawn up, it hadn't been thought necessary because there were five owners.

Above Dan Frisk lived Mariya Christodolou, a woman of

82

Greek Cypriot descent but born and raised in England. She was about thirty and called herself a designer, though no one knew, even in the most general terms, what it was that she designed. She had financial difficulties; her mortgage payments were often late or in arrears, and extracting money from her for the expenses of the common parts was always difficult, like prolonged labour.

As far as such payments were concerned, she had an ally in Mr Hashemi, who also refused them, almost as yet another matter of principle, until the last possible moment. He always denied that this was because of financial difficulties: instead, he examined the accounts minutely, and if he found a discrepancy of a few pence he magnified it into evidence of large-scale fraud and malversation.

'I pay not cheats and thieves,' he would say, but at the last possible, finely judged moment, he did.

Ms Christodolou, whose large brown eyes were emphasised by heavy black makeup and who also had streaks of gold, not natural, running through her auburn hair, was a woman of extravagant emotion apparently the consequence of her allegedly artistic temperament. She liked drama, and to this end she was a creator of crises. She said she had hot Mediterranean blood in her veins, though her father ran a fish-and-chip shop in the suburbs and her mother was a social worker. But her supposed hot blood was both an excuse in advance and an explanation for her emotional outbursts, often occasioned by her torrid but short-lived affairs with a succession of patently unsuitable lovers whom in the end she always accused of exploiting her.

She detested Mr Khorasami two floors below. She thought

he was a lecher who undressed her with his eyes. Perhaps this was not surprising given his wife's appearance. She had never been beautiful but was now positively ugly and was reputed to be shrewish. This, however, was not Ms Christodolou's affair. She had a right not to be leered at by a man old enough, almost, to be her father. She avoided him as far as possible, but sometimes meeting him as she descended to the entrance of the house was inevitable. He would pass the time of day with her, but she would cut him dead, as if he had been guilty of something. Her hostility puzzled Mr Khorasami: in his own opinion, he had done nothing to merit it.

Ms Christodolou's relations with Mr Seferis, who lived above her, were if anything even more strained. Mr Seferis, a shy and retiring bachelor approaching forty, was an actuary more at ease with a page of figures than with the human beings to whom they referred. Notwithstanding his modesty, which no one who met him failed to remark upon, Ms Christodolou thought him stuck-up and arrogant because he was from the Greek mainland and therefore (according to her) considered those of Cypriot origin, including herself, to be of inferior stock. As if this were not bad enough, there was also the question of damp. According to Ms Christodolou, the patches of damp that appeared on her walls from time to time, like an intermittent rash on a sensitive skin, were caused by leaks in Mr Seferis's plumbing upstairs, but according to Mr Seferis they were caused by Ms Christodolou's habit of lying in a hot bath for hours on end with all the windows of her flat firmly shut. Ms Christodolou now bitterly regretted having once told Mr Seferis that she liked such baths 'to chill out', as she put it. She little thought that he would one day use this information against her. But at the time she had been particularly stressed by her then boyfriend, Clyde, and she had to confide in someone or she would have burst. Clyde virtually drove her to the bath, to which she added lavender bath salts.

Once, Ms Christodolou sent Mr Seferis a letter, written by a friend who was studying law after having been a hairdresser, couched in legalistic terms and threatening him with action unless he repaired his plumbing and paid for the necessary repairs to Ms Christodolou's flat. Mr Seferis did not answer it and threw it away. Ms Christodolou believed that Mr Seferis was denying his responsibilities, thereby taking advantage of the vulnerability of a single woman; Mr Seferis thought that she was trying to redecorate her flat at his expense. She would have liked a more open quarrel with him, but he was a difficult man to quarrel with, so retiring was he. Whenever she approached him, he said, 'Excuse me, Ms Christodolou, I'm very busy at the moment and have a lot of work to do.' This gave her no time to break down in tears as she would have liked to do. It was very frustrating. Tears for her were what aperients are to people obsessed by their bowels.

Once a year, all the owners of Number 17 held a general assembly to discuss matters of interest common to them all as owners. Dan Frisk did not attend, even if he were in the country and in residence. He joked that he had had enough of conflict in his work, but the truth was that questions such as whether the hallway needed re-painting and if so in what colour (keeping it the same, or a change, such as the mauve that Ms Christodolou favoured) bored him by their triviality. When you regularly dice with death, anything less than survival seems of no importance.

That left the four of them to decide matters. Mr Seferis chaired the meeting because it was obvious that he was the most level-headed, conciliatory and business-like of any of them, a fact which even Ms Christodolou recognised. Mr Seferis drew up the agenda and always started with uncontentious subjects, so that at least something was agreed. Even then, Ms Christodolou tried to sow dissension, for example by suggesting, for no obvious reason, that they should change their insurance broker; but Mr Seferis cut her short by telling her that she was perfectly at liberty to search for new brokers if she so wished, knowing full well that very idea would be anathema to her, beside which there was no time to do it because the premium was due in ten days.

There were, however, more difficult questions to settle, for example that of the plane tree, splendid in itself, that grew in close proximity to the front of the house and not only might be undermining the foundations of the house but whose branches and leaves had now spread and brushed against the front window of Ms Christodolou's flat.

'The constant scratching is terrible,' she said. 'I can't sleep at night because of it' — though she slept mainly in the morning. 'It's like a cat clawing on glass to get in.'

Obviously, the offending branch would have to be cut, but by whom and at whose expense?

'It is the council,' said Mr Hashemi.

Everything was the council's responsibility in Mr Hashemi's opinion: that way, there would be no demands for money.

Once again, Mr Seferis explained that he had already approached the council, who had replied that, since some of the tree's roots were under Number 17's narrow strip of land between the house and the street, the responsibility to keep the tree under control was that of the owners.

'This is not justice,' said Mr Hashemi, his tone rising to a shriek.

'It's not a question of justice,' said Mr Seferis. 'It's a question of the regulations. We can't alter them.'

'This is worse than Shah!'' exclaimed Mr Hashemi, forgetting that he was supposed to have been tortured.

'Something's got to be done,' said Ms Christodolou. 'I can't sleep because of it.'

'Get the branch cut, then,' said Mr Khorasami, with a faint, malicious smile because he knew that she had no money.

'It's a collective responsibility, not mine alone,' she said. 'The roots are in our land.'

'But the branch is at your window,' said Mr Khorasami. 'It is your problem.'

Mr Seferis, on this occasion, was on Ms Christodolou's side.

'I think we have a duty to cut the branch,' he said.

'Ms Christodolou hasn't paid her annual subscription,' said Mr Khorasami.

'I'm not the only one,' she said.

'Until you have,' said Mr Khorasami, speaking directly to her, 'I don't see why we should cut your branch.'

The discussion petered out without resolution. Nobody believed anyway that Ms Christodolou could not sleep because of the branch. Sometimes she would stagger down the stairs at midday, her eyes bleary from sleep and having just woken, to collect her post. She had obviously slept very well.

'Any other business?' asked Mr Seferis, having run through his agenda and dreading what was to come.

'The cupboard under the stairs,' said Mr Hashemi.

'We discussed it last year,' said Mr Khorasami.

'It's the same,' said Mr Hashemi. 'It is of all of us, but only one man use it.' He stared at his neighbour accusingly.

'I agree,' said Ms Christodolou. 'The cupboard is a common part. We should all have use of it. '

'I have had the use of it ever since I moved in,' said Mr Khorasami, 'when there was no one else here. No one objected until Mr Hashemi moved in.'

'That was because we didn't know it was there,' said Ms Christodolou.

'Nonsense!' said Mr Khorasami. 'It was obvious it was there. 'What did you think the door was for? A door under the stairs is obviously a cupboard.'

'What do you keep in there anyway?' asked Mr Hashemi angrily.

'None of your business,' replied Mr Khorasami. 'What is it to you?'

'Don't you speak to me like this!' said Mr Hashemi.

'Gentlemen, gentlemen!' intervened Mr Seferis. 'Let us remain calm.'

'What use is the cupboard to you anyway?' asked Mr Khorasami, looking first at Ms Christodolou and then at Mr Hashemi. 'If you divide it up, there is no space for anything.'

'Then why don't we each have use of it for a year in rotation?' said Ms Christodolou, whose only interest in the cupboard was in the conflict it generated.

'A good idea!' said Mr Hashemi.

'And who's going to arrange that?' asked Mr Khorasami.

'Mr Seferis could do it,' said Ms Christodolou.

'I'm afraid not,' said Mr Seferis, foreseeing the difficulties.

'Anyway,' said Mr Khorasami, 'it's only of use to me because it's on my floor. If anyone else had it, they would have to drag things up and down the stairs and damage them.'

'They wouldn't be heavy,' said Ms Christodolou. 'You said yourself that the cupboard was small.'

'Especially when divided into five,' said Mr Khorasami.

Mr Hashemi shouted. The meeting was held in Mr Seferis's flat on the top floor, which fortunately did not relay sound. But Mr Hashemi was not pleased. He wanted the world to know that a terrible injustice was being done to him.

'I had enough!' he screamed. 'Enough, enough!' he stood up. 'I do something.' And he rushed out.

Now there were only three of them, so a majority vote was possible, at least in theory. But Ms Christodolou was against taking a vote, because she said it would be more like a coup d'état than a democratic decision. Anyone could win votes by preventing interested parties from voting. But Mr Khorasami was in favour of a vote: he said that Mr Hashemi had left the meeting of his own accord, no one had forced or even asked him to go, and that he should take the consequences. It was time for him to grow up.

Ms Christodolou knew that she could not win, and Mr Khorasami that he could not lose. The situation was pleasing to Mr Seferis because he could abstain and still Mr Khorasami could not be forced to relinquish the cupboard. If Mr Hashemi had still been present and a vote taken, Mr Seferis would have had to vote with Mr Khorasami because he preferred Mr Hashemi as an enemy to Mr Khorasami. Abstention would mean that he was neither's enemy. Having been bullied at school because he was small and clever, Mr Seferis was too timid to make enemies if he could avoid doing so.

The meeting broke up. In principle, Mr Khorasami was safe for another year in his use of the cupboard. He knew, of course, that Hashemi would not give up. He might even try to use unconstitutional means to advance his ends. The price of the continued use of the cupboard was eternal vigilance.

Two weeks after the meeting, Mr Khorasami witnessed Mr Hashemi and Ms Christodolou in secret, or secretive, conference on the stairs. What could they be talking about except the cupboard? A sexual liaison could be ruled out. Ms Christodolou's taste in men did not run to older men, rather the reverse, and not even money (of which Hashemi was in any case short) would compensate for his unattractiveness. You had only to think of Mr Hashemi with his clothes off to shudder. No, it must be the cupboard that was the subject of their whispering together, which moreover, they abandoned as soon as they realised that they were observed.

A few days later, Mr Khorasami was leaving the front door to the house just as Mr Hashemi was entering. The tiles on the steps leading up to the front door were glistening after rain. They, too, had long been a matter of contention between the owners of Number 17. Mr Seferis said that they were slippery and that in the event of someone slipping and breaking his leg or worse, they might be liable because the insurance (whose premium in any case was in arrears, because of Ms Christodolou's tardiness) wouldn't cover them. The insurance company would claim that the accident had been foreseeable and therefore preventable and was therefore the fault of the client's negligence, but Ms Christodolou, who wanted to justify or at least extenuate her failure to pay, said that the tiles on the steps had been there for a hundred years and no one had broken his leg on them yet.

'How do you know?' Mr Khorasami had asked, siding as usual with Mr Seferis. 'Have you been here for a hundred years?'

'That is no way to speak,' said Mr Hashemi, turning gallant.

A vote had been taken, inconclusive as ever, as a result of which the tiles continued to glisten after the rain.

'Be careful on the steps,' said Mr Khorasami to Mr Hashemi. 'We don't want to be sued, do we?' His sarcasm infuriated Mr Hashemi.

'Mind your business,' he said, and pushed past him, knocking his elbow as he did so. Mr Khorasami ostentatiously brushed his sleeve, as if he had been touched by something unclean that had left a trace on it.

A somewhat greater tussle occurred between them a few days later. Mr Khorasami had replaced the older, smaller padlock that secured the cupboard by a larger and more solid one. It had a combination lock and was now attached to a much stronger latch on the door. It was impossible not to notice it, and Mr Hashemi was furious. When by chance he had met Mr Seferis as he returned from work one evening, he more or less cornered him.

'We need meeting,' he said, obviously agitated.

'What about?' asked Mr Seferis.

'Look!' said Mr Hashemi, pointing with his trembling finger at the gleaming padlock. 'Look!'

Mr Seferis looked, following the direction of Mr Hashemi's

finger as a dog follows the gaze of its master.

'Look!' Mr Hashemi repeated, and went up to the cupboard door. He flicked the padlock contemptuously with his forefinger and it rattled against the cupboard door.

At that moment, Mr Khorasami emerged from the front door of his flat.

'What are you doing?' he demanded to know and approached Mr Hashemi.

'Peder sag!' said Mr Hashemi (Son of a dog!)

'Mourmi bukho!' replied Mr Khorasami (Eat bullets!)

Mr Seferis decided to take action.

'Gentlemen!' he said, approaching them.

'He is damaging our property!' said Mr Hashemi.

'I am protecting my things,' said Mr Khorasami. 'From possible thieves.'

'He is accusing us all.'

'Not all, only some. He is like a child,' said Mr Khorasami, pointing to Mr Hashemi.

Mr Seferis suggested that they retire to their respective flats. Sulkily, but with hostile glances at each other, they complied.

It was a truce rather than a peace. A week later, Mr Hashemi emerged from his flat at about six in the morning (it was still dark) and climbed the stairs to the ground floor. He was in his socks to ensure that he made no noise. This was not logical, because it was inevitable that he would make some noise with the hacksaw that he took with him.

Reaching the cupboard door, he knelt down and began to apply the hacksaw to the arm of the padlock. Progress was very slow, and the hacksaw made more noise than Mr Hashemi had anticipated. He paused, as if an interval of silence would somehow cancel out the noise that he had already made. He did not see Mr Khorasami come out of his front door, still in his pyjamas.

'What are you doing?' he said. It wasn't really a question.

'It is our property,' said Mr Hashemi. 'You give it back.'

Mr Khorasami approached Mr Hashemi, who was now struggling to his feet. He pushed Mr Hashemi, who fell back like an overturned beetle. Mr Khorasami laughed, though not mirthfully. Then he turned to go back into his flat.

'I'm calling the police,' he said.

Fury made Mr Hashemi agile. He managed to spring to his feet, leaving the hacksaw on the ground. He had brought a knife with him for just such an eventuality. He stabbed Mr Khorasami in the back with all his strength.

Mr Khorasami did not die, but Mr Hashemi went to prison. Both the basement and the ground floor flats were sold, the first because of financial necessity, the second because of its unhappy associations. The cupboard under the stairs was vacated, but none of the other three owners wanted to use it.

The ground floor flat sold first. Its new owner, Mr DiAngelo, moved some of his surplus belongings into it.

Reputation

The small town of Hobsford was behind the times, which was why old people retired there and young people left it as soon as they were able. Its centre, at least, with its Jacobean market hall, was still recognisable from photographs more than a century and a quarter old. The war memorial in the public gardens round its ruined castle, dedicated to our glorious dead, listed members of families still prominent in the town, dynasties of ironmongers, butchers, auctioneers and estate agents. Some of them, their ancestors having bought the surrounding farmland, had become a kind of local aristocracy. Even the town's plumbing was still performed by a Goodson, the fourth of that name.

Absence of change is never absolute, of course; change is inevitable and therefore, according to the Reverend Herbert Longstreet, the vicar of one of the two ancient churches of the town (the other now deconsecrated), to be welcomed and celebrated as part of God's providence. That is why he wanted to turn the churchyard of St Olav's, whose tombstones had already been removed to prevent accidents after someone tripped on one of them and sprained his ankle, into a car-park, paying except for congregants who would receive a special ticket on arrival in the church, dispensing thereby with the charges. The car-park, said the Reverend Longstreet, would encourage the disabled to attend the church, or at least remove a difficulty for them to do so, but a coalition of traditionalists and atheists claimed that it was really a revenue-raising scheme, especially on Saturdays when it was difficult to find spaces to park during the weekly market.

The Reverend Longstreet also wanted to remove the ancient carved pews of the church to make the church 'more user friendly', especially for community activities such as dances, bingo and round-table discussions. The pews were by no means comfortable to sit on. Youth, he said, were intimidated by the rows of seats that were uncomfortable even when covered with removable cushions. The Church, he said, was a place which should welcome everyone, which was why he wanted to replace the pews with aluminium-framed plastic chairs which were reasonable in price if you bought them in quantity and were easy to place in any manner necessary. The chairs would bring the church back to the centre of the town's life, where it belonged.

The Reverend Longstreet's face, which shone with the reflected light of God's love as the moon shines with the reflected light of the sun, was nevertheless not much seen around the town. It was rumoured, though without much evidence, that he was ambitious for advancement in the church, regarding Hobsford as but a steppingstone to a bishop's seat, never mind of which diocese. Sometimes, however, he would appear in a soutane, gliding rather than walking down the High Street, with a smile for everyone, even

— or perhaps especially — for the Romanian gypsy beggar who regularly took up her station outside the little, local mini-supermarket that was open till midnight, much patronised at that hour by the local drunks in search of cheap, strong cider. She, the Romanian gypsy beggar, sold individual roses that no one wanted but that made some feel guiltily uncharitable if they did not buy, even though it was strongly suspected that her source of supply was the rather beautiful Victorian municipal cemetery on the outskirts of the town. No one knew where she went after her day was over: she vanished, as did the waiters of the town's three Indian restaurants.

All visitors to the town were inclined to believe that it was free from what are called social problems, with no crime or disorder. It was true that, considering that the town's police station had closed several years earlier, there was little crime apart from shoplifting by the younger residents of a housing estate built on the periphery to alleviate the problem of unemployment in the nearest, much larger town. As for disorder, it consisted of occasional Saturday night brawls outside one of the town's many pubs, usually attributed by the townspeople to the intrusion of outsiders. Compared with most places, however, there was little to complain of or reason to fear.

George and Mary Reed decided to retire to Hobsford. He had been a lecturer in biochemistry and she a teacher of piano. They had thought long and hard about the move, weighed up its pros and cons, but finally decided that the former outweighed the latter. They would be relieved to escape at last the atmosphere of incipient riot of the large city in which they had lived for thirty years. Hobsford had few cultural resources, perhaps, but if they were honest, they had availed themselves of such resources in the city infrequently, so that their benefits remained somewhat theoretical, more a kind of insurance policy than an actual possession. And they were old and mature enough to realise that there are no advantages in this life without disadvantages.

They bought a small Georgian house around a close around one of the churches, a sandstone edifice so heavily restored that hardly any of it was original, though it still had a splendid chapterhouse. Apart from the absence of church life, and the fact that the Victorian rectory had been converted into the offices of a chartered accountant, you might have thought that you had stepped into the pages of a novel by Anthony Trollope.

As Trollope knew, it is not given to human beings to live in complete harmony, however pleasant their surroundings, that is to say without gossip or thinking ill of one another, and the fact that the Perkins, who lived at number 7, had managed to secure for themselves three parking permits when two was the maximum allowed for any household, aroused suspicions of deep corruption or illicit influence in high municipal places, but those suspicions were uttered only sotto voce, and of course no one spoke of them to the Perkins themselves.

The Reeds, who knew no one in the town when they arrived, desired to fit into the town without making themselves conspicuous. They had been told by friends in the city before they moved that small country towns were small-minded, their populations bigoted, ignorant and stand-offish, but they found this to be untrue, the mere prejudice of the lengthily-educated who, though theoretically open-minded, secretly despised everyone who was not like themselves. They had been told of the horrors of gossip and intrusiveness in such a place, in which it was impossible to say or do anything without exciting notice and without the whole town knowing and commenting on it; but, on the contrary, they found the recognition in the streets and shops, the feeling that they were no longer a nameless face in a crowd, to be pleasant. They were surprised by how soon and how many people would now pass the time of day with them.

They joined the local historical society, both out of interest and to make acquaintances. Hobsford was an ancient borough and had once been an important place. It was on the last reach of the river on which it was situated that was navigable by boats of size enough to bring worthwhile cargo, up to the coming of the railways. And though the Reeds were no longer young, they brought to the society almost the breath of youth by comparison with most of the membership, about a half of which wore hearing-aids during the monthly talks in the town's undistinguished Community Hall, a flat-roofed edifice constructed in the 1950s on the edge of the town, inclined to damp and mould and impossible to heat. Everyone had to wrap up warm for the winter meetings, but the chilliness was able to penetrate any amount of wool. Far from putting off the members, however, the discomfort of the place only encouraged them, acting as proof of their devotion to the history of their town.

The talks of the society were very various and some of them were frankly dull. Since a goodly third of the audience fell asleep as soon as the lights were dimmed and were wakened only if they snored, this perhaps did not matter. There was no connection, admittedly, between the quality or interest of the talk and the somnolence it induced, and even subjects of exceptional interest, such as the history and biographies of the stationmasters of Hobsford (before the line was closed down forty-five years earlier, now sorely missed) failed to keep everyone awake.

The chairman of the society, it so happened, was the Reeds' next-door neighbour, Mr Arthur Greenfield. In the past he had been town mayor, and there was a photograph of him as such in the town hall, dignified in his red, fur-trimmed robe and golden chain of office (the fur-trimming had since been removed in deference to, or fear of, the defenders of animals' rights). Practically everyone who stood for the town council was elected, because the position of councillor was onerous without honour, and Mr Greenfield had long since withdrawn from public life. Everyone who had ever served on the council was suspected, ex officio as it were, of having feathered his own nest.

Not that Mr Greenfield needed to feather his own nest: he was very rich from having sold his family business. In the eyes of many, however, this only strengthened his reputation for dishonesty, for how could one become rich without dishonesty? His failure to flaunt his wealth was another ground for suspicion, for if he had acquired it honestly, why his modest train of life, and why did he not live in grander fashion and on a larger scale? Not that it would have escaped adverse comment if he had done so, for then he would have been accused of parading his good fortune by means of ostentation before the less prosperous of the town. But the fact that he did not draw attention to himself drew attention to himself. For many, then, there was no correct way for him to believe, once he had committed the original sin of being richer than they.

His longstanding chairmanship of the Hobsford Historical Society, an elective post, was not the consequence of personal popularity but of the reluctance of anyone else to fill it. Whatever one might say about successful businessmen, they were good at organising, besides which it was as well to have a rich man involved in the society should it run into financial difficulties or the treasurer run off with the funds. True, this seemed unlikely, since the treasurer, Miss Farmer, was the retired former headmistress of the town's primary school, who treated the members as if they were mildly misbehaved, small children who required, and actually liked, firm but kindly handling. She it was who manned the desk at the entrance to the hall on the evening of the meetings, upbraiding those who were later with their subscriptions. She was also the one who took the money for the tea and biscuits served after the talks, again gently upbraiding those who did not proffer the right change, reminding them that she was not minding a shop. The sums that passed through her hands were not such as to tempt a respectable, elderly spinster to a new career in crime, but appearances could be deceptive. The last treasurer had likewise been an old lady of impeccable credentials, a sub-postmistress of many years' service, but at the end of her tenure (coincident with her death), yawning gaps were found in the accounts. This was hushed up, and Mr Greenfield made up the deficit, which was just as well since the old lady was discovered to have been demented and the missing money found secreted all over her house after her death, in tea-caddies, biscuit tins, a pencil case, and between the pages of books. Mr Greenfield declined to be reimbursed, but since this was unknown to the public, it did nothing to improve or repair his reputation. If it had been known, of course, it would only have confirmed that he had a need to ingratiate himself with the townspeople: what other explanation for such generosity could there be?

Naturally, the townspeople were polite enough to Mr Greenfield's face and even chatted with him pleasantly in the street. But he knew, and they knew, that all the time they spoke to him there were arrières pensées. Even passing the time of day with him was not without them.

The Reeds, of course, did not share them and at first did not even know that they existed. Their relations with their new neighbour were cordial, and he seemed to them not only affable but the kind of man with whom they would like to make friends, or at least (for they had reached the age at which new friendships were not easily made) be on friendly terms with. Mr Greenfield was a man of diverse interests, from birdwatching to literature, particularly of the nineteenth century. It so happened that the latter was an interest of Mr Reed's also.

The Reeds had their own friends, of course, but they had either remained near to their old home or moved away to disparate parts of the country. They could maintain their old friendships only indirectly; actual visits would be sporadic at best. Never in any case much involved in a social whirl, they were not natural hermits either. They needed congenial company from time to time, and Mr Greenfield was fortunately to hand.

'We're very lucky,' said Mr Reed to his wife, 'when you think whom we could have had as a neighbour!'

'Or spouse,' said Mrs Reed, smiling.

'We always underestimate the part that chance plays in our lives.'

'We always have to play the hand we've been dealt.'

'But we do sometimes have a choice in the hand that we hold.'

'But only with the hand we've already been dealt.'

'Careful, or you'll soon be back to the Garden of Eden as the explanation of everything.'

Mr Greenfield was a widower. He was several years older than the Reeds, though still active and well-preserved and apt to be considered an old man. The Reeds thought of inviting him to dinner.

'I'm not sure it would be a good idea,' said Mrs Reed.

'Why?' asked Mr Reed.

'It might embarrass him. He would feel obliged to ask us back, and perhaps he can't cook, at least not well enough to have guests.'

'You're right, I hadn't thought of that.'

They decided to invite him instead to dinner in a restaurant. The town had several restaurants, all of them within walking distance. By stealthy enquiry, Mrs Reed discovered that Mr Greenfield had no special dietary requirements, as they are called these days, and so they invited him to what was reputed to be the best restaurant in the town, in an ancient half-timbered pub, in which, according to the menu, everything was 'sourced locally'.

The dinner went well. The food was good and happily they

drank in the same moderation. Conversation was easy. The Reeds spoke of themselves and their reasons for having moved to Hobsford.

'The city was becoming unliveable,' said Mr Reed. 'Crowded, dirty, noisy.'

'And unsafe,' added Mrs Reed. 'That was the straw that broke the camel's back.'

'In the morning, we would find used condoms or needles in the street, sometimes in our front garden. And it used to be a quiet, residential road.'

'We were opposite a church, funnily enough.'

'Just like now,' said Mr Greenfield, laughing quietly.

'It was completely different in the city,' said Mr Reed. 'They stuffed their empty cans of strong beer in the laurel bushes around the church and scratched parked cars out of spite, especially the expensive ones. We were afraid to go out at night.'

'It's so quiet here by comparison,' said Mrs Reed. 'And people are so friendly and polite.'

'There are fewer young people,' said Mr Reed, by way of explanation.

'They leave,' said Mr Greenfield. 'There's nothing for them to do here.'

'The students, they were the worst,' said Mrs Reed. 'Many of the houses had been turned into student lodgings. They had no consideration for others. They played their music so loud that the ground shook. You could feel it coming up through your legs.'

'At all times of the day and night,' said Mr Reed.

'And they took drugs all the time. That brought the drug

dealers, of course.'

'You could see them quite openly,' said Mr Reed. 'They didn't bother to hide it. The police did nothing, of course.'

'They weren't from bad homes, the students,' said Mrs Reed. 'If you spoke to them as individuals they were quite all right. If you complained about the noise, they would promise to make less, but they didn't keep it for long. The next day it was just as bad.'

'We had years of it. We couldn't stand it any longer.'

'What the future'll be, I dread to think.'

'Perhaps they'll grow out of it,' said Mr Greenfield. 'After all, we did.'

'I don't think we were ever like that,' said Mrs Reed. 'At least, not as bad. We didn't take drugs.'

'And in those days, drugs were less strong,' said Mr Reed, with professional authority. 'For example, cannabis had only three or four per cent active component. Now it's ten or even fifteen per cent. It has a completely different effect on the mind.'

'Some of them go mad,' said Mrs Reed. 'I suppose it serves them right, in a way.'

'But that doesn't help us,' said her husband. 'I don't know what we can do about it, it's gone too far. Anyway, there's nothing we can do about it, except move away.

The main dishes came.

'Ah, this is excellent,' said Mr Reed, trying his.

Mrs Reed's was also good.

They spoke little while they ate, and afterwards the subject of conversation changed. The Reeds spoke of their children, of whom they were proud.

'Sam's in the City,' said Mrs Reed. 'I don't really understand what he does there. He's tried to explain, but I still don't understand.'

'He studied maths at university,' said Mr Reed. 'They all went into the City afterwards. They all earn fantastic salaries straight away, or soon afterwards at any rate. They're recruited even before they've left university.'

'Sam could retire already if he wanted to, and he's only in his thirties. Of course, I don't really think it's right, but I suppose you can't blame them for going into the City.'

'And your daughter?' asked Mr Greenfield. They had told her that they had a son and a daughter.

'She's a teacher. French. She always wanted to teach in a school in an inner city. She has a strong social conscience. But it was impossible. They wouldn't even learn English, let alone French. She had to take a job in a private school, or she would have gone mad. At least they are prepared to learn.'

'She's married to a surgeon,' said Mr Reed, with a strong accent of approval. 'He's just got his first consultancy.'

'He specialises in knees,' said Mrs Reed. 'There's a lot of money in knees, apparently. That's all he does, knees. I'm worried that he'll get bored with them, the same thing day in, day out, for years.'

'But things change all the time,' said her husband. 'Techniques improve, and don't forget that he's an inventor. He tells us that he's developing a new pin, or something, that will revolutionise knee surgery.'

'I have a bit of knee trouble,' said Mr Greenfield, and they started to talk of the minor ailments consequent upon advancing age.

When the bill came, the Reeds insisted upon paying it. Mr Greenfield said that it would be his turn next time, but the Reeds said that it would not be fair or just, since they were two and he was only one. They agreed that, from now on they would share the bill, thus establishing that their dinners together would be regular, weekly in fact.

They walked back together the short distance to their adjacent houses and bade each other goodnight.

Once safely indoors, Mr and Mrs Reed started to talk about Mr Greenfield, though with lowered voices just in case.

'I liked him,' said Mr Reed. 'He was easy, straightforward, had no side.'

'Yes,' said his wife. 'I agree. But did you notice something about him?'

Mrs Reed was always noticing things that her husband did not, sometimes even things that were not there.

'What?' he asked.

'He didn't tell us anything about himself.'

'Perhaps he's just reserved.'

'We told him a lot about ourselves. We don't even know whether he has any children.'

'Well, it was the first time we've ever really spoken to him.'

But in fact, he continued to speak very little of himself. They discovered that he was widowed early and had no children but very little else. He had a brother in Manchester whom he did not see very often.

'He must be lonely,' said Mrs Reed.

'He seems perfectly content,' said Mr Reed. 'Some people don't care for company.'

Next door to them on the other side, also in a Georgian

house, lived Mrs and Mrs Soothill. They were retired too, he from accountancy, she from district nursing. Although in his time he must have earned a good deal more than she, he seemed to be but her shadow. He hardly spoke in her presence, and then only to agree with or confirm what she said. There was such an indefiniteness about him that he seemed almost more of an absence than a presence. One noticed what he wasn't more than what he was.

Her presence was more than double his absence, however. She made it her business to know everything that was going on in the town and had definite opinions about it, generally unfavourable. And yet she was not unkindly. She was the pillar of many worthy organisations but did not confine her good works to them and performed personal services for people who needed them: for example, doing the shopping for old people on their return from hospital. She did this inconspicuously, from genuine goodness of heart and not from desire for praise. She could be relied to step in where others would not. She had what she called standards.

She developed the habit of 'popping in' next door to her new neighbours. She said that Stanley, her husband, could spare her for a few minutes, as if he were some kind of domestic dictator. She was like a bee whose pollen was gossip and who distilled the nectar of information into the honey of disapproval. She did not so much walk as bustle. She began many of her sentences, by saying 'If you ask me…'

You could tell when she had something particularly scandalous or disgraceful to impart by the solemn expression on her face from which she could not altogether exclude the pleasurable excitement she felt in what she had to say. She was easily outraged, which meant that her life had a sense of meaning and purpose. She was a local patriot and believed that many of the town's ills were imported from outside, for example from the nearest city, notwithstanding that she had a low opinion of most of the town's inhabitants.

'They came last week and smashed the bus shelter in the High Street,' she told Mrs Reed one morning, quivering with pleasant indignation.

'Who?' asked Mrs Reed.

'Louts from the city. They come here drinking and vandalise the town.' A single incident became a regular occurrence in Mrs Soothill's mind. 'They should do something about it.'

There were two theys in Mrs Soothill's estimation: they who did bad things, and they who should stop them. It was not always clear who they were in person.

Another morning, Mrs Soothill arrived in a more subdued, even sombre, mood. Evidently, she had something important to say. She said so herself.

'Everyone's noticed that you've become friendly with Mr Greenfield,' she began.

Of course they had. Hobsford was the kind of town in which everyone noticed everything. This was for good and ill. It meant that you couldn't move without being seen or even observed, but it also meant that everything you did was of interest to someone, thus lending significance or importance to it. You were never just an ant in a heap.

'Yes,' said Mrs Reed, 'we have dinner every Friday night with him. We find him pleasant company.'

'Oh, I daresay,' said Mrs Soothill, her voice trailing off into implication.

'What do you mean?'

Mrs Soothill wiggled a little on the kitchen chair, as if reluctant to speak.

'Well,' she said, 'you know that he doesn't have a very good reputation in the town.'

Mrs Reed didn't know it. She was surprised.

'In what way?' she asked.

Mrs Soothill remained solemnly silent for a few moments, as if struggling with herself as to what to say. Then she managed to convey that she spoke only with reluctance.

'Where did his money come from?' she said, finally.

'I haven't the faintest idea. It's none of my business. Where did it come from?' Mrs Reed's tone was fainty satirical.

'Ah, that's the question. He had a family business, of course, but he sold it years ago. He couldn't have lived off the proceeds this long.'

'Perhaps he invested them very well.'

'Perhaps.' It was clear that Mrs Soothill believed no such thing. 'Of course, he inherited a lot of money from his wife.'

'Well, there you are then.'

'In a way,' said Mrs Soothill. 'In a way.'

'What do you mean?'

Mrs Soothill was usually pretty plain-speaking, but now she was skirting round the subject like a vulture hopping around a dying animal.

'There are people who think that there was something fishy about the inheritance, the way he inherited it.'

'It's quite normal for a man to inherit from his wife. And vice versa of course.'

'Naturally. But then…'

'But then what?'

'I'd better not say any more. I don't want to turn you against him or inform. I just thought I'd let you know.' Mrs Soothill rose to go, having fulfilled her duty. 'I must be getting on,' she said, glancing at the kitchen clock. 'My husband will be wondering where I've got to.'

She spoke as if she were under his thumb, and bustled out, saying at the door 'I'd be careful of him if I were you.'

'What did she mean?' asked Mr Reed, when his wife relayed to him her conversation with Mrs Soothill.

'I don't know. I suppose she's trying to create a mystery out of nothing. In towns like this where nothing ever happens, they make up things to persuade themselves that they aren't bored.'

They continued to have dinner every Friday night with Mr Greenfield.

'How are you getting on with your neighbour?' asked Mrs Soothill, midway between reproach and enquiry.

'Very well,' said Mrs Reed. 'He's amusing. He knows a lot about local history.'

'His family has lived here a long time.'

'He doesn't talk about his family.'

'He wouldn't. I'm not surprised.'

There was insinuation in Mrs Soothill's words, without any indication of what she was insinuating.

One day, Mr Reed was rooting around in a local antique, or bric-a-brac, shop, a cavernous establishment which was cold inside even during heatwaves. The smell of a special kind of dust, unique to such places, was permanently in the air.

Among the items for sale were a few books, forlorn on some shelves in the corner, where they had evidently remained for years. It was highly unlikely that anyone would ever want the fifth volume of an eighteenth-century clergyman's collected sermons with the front board missing and many of the pages scribbled over by a naughty bored child with a red pencil. The stock on the shelves rarely changed, but sometimes there would be a small infusion of new titles as a newly bereaved widow tried to disembarrass herself of her husband's books. Mr Reed was a keen hunter of bargains.

On this occasion, his eye was caught by a title he had not noticed before: The Hobsford Horror. It had been published more than forty years earlier, when Mr Reed was a young man and Hobsford meant nothing to him. He was intrigued: Hobsford and horror seemed ill-assorted.

He could hardly believe his eyes. More than forty years ago, the then Mrs Greenfield, pregnant, had been kidnapped by a local builder who had gone bankrupt, according to him because the town council had failed to pay him for the work he had done. He was bitter and angry and hoped to make a fortune at a stroke, in order to escape to South America. Kidnap for ransom seemed to him the perfect solution to his problems.

He planned it well. At the time the Greenfields lived in an isolated farmhouse outside the town. He had only to wait for Mr Greenfield to go to work and for the cleaning lady to leave for there to be no witnesses. The kidnapper took Mrs Greenfield, bound and trussed, to a disused army blockhouse fifty miles away, across the lines of another police force. He knew that the two police forces were rivals and would not cooperate in any investigation: they hated each other much more than they hated criminals.

But the handing over of the ransom demanded went badly. Of course, the kidnapper made it a condition of the deal, as he called it, that the police should not be involved: if they were, the deal was off and the kidnapped woman dead. But a police helicopter flew over the scene of the proposed site of the handover of the ransom money, and the kidnapper panicked. He returned to the army blockhouse where he had secreted Mrs Greenfield. Convinced that he was being followed, he shot her with his shotgun, which he then turned on himself. The bodies were not found for two months.

Mr Reed bought the book, of course, and took it home, where he and his wife read it carefully. They said nothing about it to Mr Greenfield, naturally: it was the kind of subject that it was for the person most concerned to broach, which he never would. They discussed the case between themselves. They agreed that Mr Greenfield's experience was of the kind that one might in time put to the back of one's mind but which would affect one's view of human existence forever. No wonder, then, that pleasant enough as he was, there was something vague, impersonal, dissociated from life about Mr Greenfield. Tragedy such as he had experienced was not to be repaired.

After they had both read the book, Mrs Soothill bustled in as usual, 'Just for a moment', as she put it. She saw the book on the kitchen dresser.

'So you know,' she said, significantly.

'Poor man!' said Mrs Reed.

Mrs Soothill gave her a meaning glance.

'His wife was pregnant at the time she was kidnapped and murdered,' said Mrs Reed. 'He lost his child as well.'

'If it was his child,' said Mrs Soothill.

'What?'

'Everyone knew at the time that she was carrying on…'

Mrs Soothill's voice reduced to a whisper. She leaned across the table.

'Everyone knew, but don't breathe a word to anyone that I told you.'

'And so?' asked Mrs Reed.

'Well,' continued Mrs Soothill, as if with reluctance, 'everyone in the town at the time thought that Mr Greenfield was in league with the kidnapper.'

'What!' exclaimed Mrs Reed.

'Yes,' said Mrs Soothill, 'and what's more, everyone still thinks it.'

'But why on earth would he…?'

'Don't forget that his wife was a wealthy woman in her own right, and in addition her life was insured. His business wasn't doing well. And then there was the pregnancy…'

'But what was the evidence?'

'It stood to reason, don't you think? Wasn't it a happy coincidence that she was kidnapped just at the right time? After all, nothing like this had ever happened before.'

'You mean, Mr Greenfield paid the kidnapper?'

'Yes, of course, that's what people think. He knew the kidnapper personally. He knew that he was a bit of a rough diamond and that he needed the money. In a town like this, we all know who the bad hats are.'

'Then why did he kill himself as well as Mrs Greenfield?'

'Why? Because he'd failed. He knew he was never going to get the ransom money, or rather, his pay-off. He knew Greenfield would want him out of the way and from his own experience how ruthless he could be. And of course, Greenfield would have to pretend to have been devastated by the loss of his wife and child-to-be. He would deny any conspiracy, of which there would be no proof.'

'But there is no proof.'

'In a town like this, we know… that's why I advise you to be careful.'

That evening was the evening for dinner with Mr Greenfield.

'You've been here for more than six months already,' he said, taking a sip of red wine. 'How do you like it?'

'We love it,' said Mrs Reed. 'No noisy neighbours, no students, no drug dealing.'

'Yes, nothing ever happens here,' said Mr Reed, with a slightly brittle emphasis.

DROWNING

Henry was a happy little boy until the day his mother announced that he was soon to have a little brother. His face darkened.

'I don't want one,' he said. 'I don't need one.'

His mother, Joanna, said, 'You'll love him, you'll see.' And she believed it.

Her prediction was not borne out, however. Henry, though only seven, was already set in his ways, or at least firmly of the belief that he should have everything his own way. Once he said that he would not do something, he would not do it. He was by nature drawn to defend his honour, which meant keeping his word. He was characterful, determined and obstinate.

He was a clever boy, too. He grasped things very quickly and was in advance of others in his class. His mind, said his father, John, was like a sponge, both absorbent and retentive. A great future was foreseen for him by his teachers, his aunts and uncles and, of course, by his parents.

But as the date of his mother's confinement approached, he grew more sullen. Sometimes he would drop things deliberately and break them, or he would sneak off and not answer to his name. His life, which had hitherto been founded on the undivided attention of his parents, had been perfectly satisfactory to him, and he saw no reason why it should change just because of the arrival of an interloper for whom he had never asked, much less agreed to.

The great day came, and Joanna went to hospital. John and she had discussed Henry's hostile attitude and agreed that it was a passing phase and that the natural affection children felt for babies, as for small furry animals, would soon overcome it. They bought him what they called a role-model book, a story in which a boy just like him, who at first detested the idea of a sibling, soon developed a passionate attachment to his baby sister. Admittedly, Henry's sibling-to-be was a brother, not a sister, but the analogy to Henry's situation was near enough and anyway was the nearest John and Joanna had been able to find. Henry called the book soppy and flung it away angrily. If his parents thought they could get round him like that, they had another think coming.

Joanna and John, but especially Joanna, were inclined to think that Nature knows best and had at first considered a birth at home. They believed that it was wrong to have turned natural processes, such as childbirth, into medical procedures with constant technical interference. Henry's attitude, however, made birth at home impossible. Almost certainly, he would have made life intolerable, slamming doors and demanding attention all the time. It was better to present him with a fait accompli.

Joanna went off to the hospital with John when her contractions could no longer be ignored. Henry was left in the care of their charming Lithuanian cleaning-lady whose English was rudimentary but who agreed to stay as long as necessary. Henry neither liked nor disliked her: he regarded her as a fact of life, though one of minor importance compared with, say, his computer.

Things went badly at the hospital. No one there paid much attention to Joanna, who was left to get on with it until suddenly there was panic. Nurses and doctors rushed around, seemingly bumping into one another, and eventually the chief was called. He reassured Joanna and John that there was nothing to worry about, and the baby, to be called Felix, was born soon afterwards under his expert direction. Felix was taken straight to intensive care, 'Just as a precaution,' the chief said. Still nothing to worry about. Perfectly routine.

Baby Felix was kept only for a week. That, said the chief, was a good sign. Felix would probably be normal.

'Probably?' asked John anxiously (Joanna had already been sent home).

'At least eighty per cent,' said the chief. He seemed to be pleased with this and evidently thought that John and Joanna ought to be grateful for it.

When baby Felix came home, Henry affected an indifference towards him. Joanna had hoped that the sight of his baby brother would arouse his protective instinct, which she believed laid within every human breast. Was it not the case that people often gathered round to coo over a baby of someone whom they did not even know? But that instinct hadn't developed in Henry yet; he was probably too young, and he looked at Felix with as much interest or affection as with which he looked at last year's discarded toy.

Even this, however, did not reflect Henry's true feelings towards baby Felix. Of course, he was not able to identify these for himself; he could only express them obliquely by his behaviour. He always referred to Felix as It.

'Don't call Felix It, darling,' said his mother. 'It's not nice. You must call him Felix.'

'Why must I, if I don't want to?' asked Henry. There was no doubt that he was clever beyond his years.

Joanna found his question not an easy one to answer, at least not convincingly.

'How would you like it if someone called you It?'

'But It doesn't care. It can't speak. It doesn't understand.'

It was true that Baby Felix was strangely inert. He didn't seem to respond to anything very much. He didn't smile or make clapping movements. He just lay there. Secretly, Joanna could understand, or thought she could understand, why Henry called Felix It. She was worried, and so was John. Baby Felix even took his feeds listlessly.

They went with him to consult a paediatrician, an amiable man on the verge of retirement. He gave the reassuring impression of having seen, heard or experienced everything before. It was evident that he knew what he was talking about.

He examined Baby Felix closely and put him through his paces, as it were. Then he took John and Joanna into a small, quiet room to talk to them in confidence. Baby Felix lay on Joanna's lap.

'I'm afraid,' said the doctor, 'that I haven't got very good news for you.'

John and Joanna looked at one another. To be honest, they

had been expecting it.

'Baby Felix is a little behind in his development,' said the doctor.

'How far behind?' asked Joanna.

'It's impossible to be precise just at the moment,' said the doctor. 'However…'

The way he let the word trail off into silence was more eloquent than anything that he could have said. And silence often speaks louder than words.

'Is it possible that he'll catch up one day?' asked John.

'Well, as you know,' replied the doctor, almost as if addressing colleagues rather than parents, 'medicine is not an exact science. Nothing in it is absolutely certain… but no,' he added, the essential appearing almost as an afterthought, 'it is almost impossible.'

'How bad will he be?' asked Joanna.

'Again, it's impossible to tell at this stage. Only time will tell.'

'But if you had to guess?'

'If I had to guess? If I had to guess (but I don't like guessing), I should say that he'll be quite severely handicapped.'

John put his hand on Joanna's knee. At any rate, they would face things together.

'Will he be able to talk, walk, feed and dress himself?' asked Joanna.

'Oh, I should think so,' said the doctor. 'Of course, that's not a promise.'

'Why is he like this?' asked John. 'Is it genetic, I mean in case we should want another child?'

'We can't rule that out without further tests,' said the

119

doctor, 'but I don't think so.'

'What, then?'

'Probably anoxic brain damage.'

'What is that?'

'Well, as you know,' he said, almost as a colleague again, 'the brain needs oxygen. During birth, the supply is particularly vulnerable, as is the brain itself. It doesn't take much to interrupt it, and if the interruption is longer than for anything but a brief moment, there is damage.'

'And how does the interruption happen?'

'Oh, there are many ways. Without reviewing the case history in great detail, it is impossible to say.'

At that moment, a nurse entered the room.

'Doctor,' she said, 'you're needed urgently in Ward Six.'

'I'll come straight away,' he said, and the nurse withdrew not having noticed, or acknowledged, the presence of John and Joanna.

'You'll excuse me,' said the doctor, getting up to go. 'I'm needed elsewhere. I'm very sorry…'

John and Joanna were left to take Baby Felix home. They were silent in the car, but both were thinking, or replaying in their minds, the same thing, the same scenes in the hospital during Felix's birth. There, surely, in the panic of the staff, the falling over each other in the desperate search of what should have been immediately to hand, was the secret of Baby Felix's current and future condition. John's thoughts turned to remedies — legal remedies, that is.

Baby Felix now grew more rapidly in size than in mind. All that he did and learned, he did and learned much later than he should have done. His speech was delayed and indistinct, fragmentary and primitive. Henry mocked him for it. No appeal to his better feelings, no cajoling, no threats of punishment, such as being sent to his room, could make him behave towards Felix with any more grace. For him, Felix remained It.

John told Joanna that he was thinking of going to law.

'What good will that do?' asked Joanna. 'What's done is done.'

'They shouldn't be able to get away with it,' said John. 'If we don't do anything, they'll never learn, and it could happen to somebody else.'

He didn't mention that the money would come in useful, because it was obvious that Baby Felix was going to need a lot of looking after and that if Joanna were ever to have a life other than looking after him, they would have to employ somebody, possibly two people, which they were unlikely to be able to afford from their own income. But John knew that Joanna would have found any mention of money to be sordid, even disgusting, and accuse him of trying to profit from the situation. Joanna was inclined to be high-minded.

Baby Felix did need a lot of attention, in fact all the attention that Joanna could give. Of course, Henry noticed this and was angry about it. He even said as much.

'Why do you have to spend so much time looking after It?' he asked Joanna one day.

'Because Felix can't do things for himself, unlike you,' she replied.

'What use is he, then?'

'Darling, people are not useful like a cup and saucer. We love them for themselves.'

121

'I don't like Felix, in fact I hate him.'

'Darling, you mustn't say things like that. Besides, it's not true.'

'It is true. He just lies there and makes a mess. He hardly speaks. He can't learn anything, not even his one times table. What's he going to be when he grows up?'

'What are you going to be when you grow up?' asked Joanna, trying to divert him from his shocking disdain for Felix. But Henry was too bright for easy diversionary tactics.

'Whatever it is, I'm not going to look after It when I grow up.'

Henry didn't really desire any more of his mother's attention; he was too grown-up already for that. It was simply that he did not want Felix to have more of it than he did.

However, this was impossible in the nature of things. It took as much effort to teach Felix to do up a button as it had taken to teach Henry, who was very quick to learn everything, to read. Felix couldn't even feed himself properly. He went to a special school for those such as he, but somehow that failed to relieve Joanna of her burden very greatly. When Felix wasn't there, away at school, she was washing, cleaning, preparing for him, and also thinking of him.

Gradually, over a few years, Henry began to misbehave. Joanna noticed that money went missing from wherever she put it. Sometimes Henry smelt of cigarettes. He made friends with the wrong crowd: the children in his school who bullied or truanted, who regarded attempts to do schoolwork properly as not only stupid but as some kind of betrayal of the young to the old. Naturally his marks suffered and from being one of the best in his class, he went to being one of the worst. He never spoke but he sneered and contradicted anything that Joanna or John said to him. He knew everything best and treated them as if, mentally, they were little better than Felix. It reached the point at which John and Joanna wouldn't have been surprised if he began to take drugs. Once or twice, they smelt alcohol on his breath.

John had contacted a lawyer with a view to suing the hospital. The lawyer explained that it wasn't enough to prove that the hospital had harmed Felix but that they had harmed him because of some error or omission.

'That should be easy enough,' said John. 'You should have seen how they panicked during the birth.'

'It won't be as easy as you think,' said the lawyer. 'First, we have to prove that the harm was caused by the hospital, and then that the hospital was at fault. These are not the same thing. And then there is the question of money.'

The lawyer presented John with a choice. Either he could pay for the proceedings himself or agree that the lawyer would double the normal fee if he won the case. It was only nominally a choice: there was no question of John funding it from his own pocket. He could afford only the initial consultation.

'The first step,' said the lawyer, 'is to obtain the hospital records.'

'That should be easy enough,' said John.

'It should be,' said the lawyer, infusing his words with meaning which John failed to take. He thought the lawyer had just agreed.

John imagined the lawyer setting to work straight away. Because his case was important to him, he thought it must be important to the lawyer. How long could it take to write a letter and reply to it? A week, perhaps, two at the most. At the end of a fortnight, he called the lawyer. It took several calls and at least two promises that he would be called back to speak to him.

'There's nothing to report yet,' said the lawyer. 'Don't worry, as soon as I have any news, I'll contact you.'

After another three weeks, John could contain himself no longer. He called again.

'Still no news, I'm afraid. I'll send them a reminder. After that...'

'After that?'

'After that, I'll start to apply some pressure.'

When he put the phone down, the lawyer dictated his first letter to the hospital.

John had not yet told Joanna that he had gone to a lawyer. He wanted first to see what came of it. After a further three weeks, he received a call from the lawyer.

'I'm afraid the hospital says that they've lost the records,' he said.

'Lost the records!'

'They say they're changing their information system, and they must have got lost in the changeover.'

'But that's ridiculous,' said John. 'They can't have lost them.'

'Oh, don't worry, it's quite normal. Losing the records is often the first line of defence. It's just a delaying tactic. They usually turn up in the end.'

'What are you going to do about it?'

'Don't worry, I'm not going to let the grass grow under our

feet. I won't let them get away with it. They'll have to find them, or else.'

This was not really an answer, but John, seething, had to accept it. He was now so worked up that he could not keep it to himself any longer: he had to tell Joanna. She was not pleased; in fact, she was angry that he had done something behind her back, without consulting her, and furthermore had concealed it for several weeks. She was almost glad, and felt vindicated, that the hospital had lost the records. It was just what she would have expected, and she hoped it would teach John a lesson. It was a waste of time and energy embroiling oneself with the law.

'I'm not giving up,' said John. Men who are not strong sometimes become obstinate. It disguises their weakness.

'You're wasting your time. It'll only make you miserable and bad-tempered.'

It was true that there were many frustrations in bringing the case. Why did everything have to take so long? The lawyer explained the next step.

'We'll have to have Professor Jones to give his opinion as to causation. He's the best in the field, of course. He's very good in the box, if it comes to that, which hopefully it won't.'

'The box?'

'The witness box under cross-examination. It's not enough to be right. You have to be convincing.'

'I see.'

'The trouble is that he's very busy. He can't provide a report for at least six months.'

'Isn't there anyone else?'

'As I said, Jones is far and away the best. He drives barristers for the other side mad. All the others are not as good, and besides they're almost as busy. We'd have to wait nearly as long for something of a much lower quality. Besides,' said the lawyer, lowering his voice almost an octave, 'in the context of litigation like this, six months is not such a long time.'

'And what if he takes even longer?'

'Another month or two won't make any difference.'

Not to him, John thought.

'And after that?' he asked.

'Well, assuming that Jones supports our case, we'll have to get an export report as to negligence.'

'Why don't we get one now to save time?'

'If Jones doesn't support our case as to causation, we're dead in the water, and there would be no point, but we'd still be stuck with the bill, and it would be us who had to pay it because we'd have lost the case.' By us, he meant him.

'So that might be another six months?'

'At least.'

And then, of course, explained the lawyer, the 'other side' would have to get its own reports. You couldn't expect them just to roll over and surrender in a case of this magnitude. The lawyer had dealt with this hospital before. They were fighters.

'But that means it could be another year,' said John, midway between interrogatory and indignation, and partaking of both.

'Oh yes, easily. But the courts are so choc-a-bloc at the moment that we wouldn't even get to court, if necessary, for three years at least. That's, of course, if we don't settle. But it's the final result that counts.'

'Settle?'

'Yes, out of court. They pay us something without admitting liability. Then everyone's happy.'

'But it was their fault.'

'Yes, yes, I know. But even if it wasn't, we'd still get paid.'

The lawyer rose, walked round his desk and patted John encouragingly on the shoulder. His manner, though he was not much older than he, was avuncular.

'Leave it to me,' he said, 'and try not to become a barrack-room lawyer. That way madness lies. You have to learn to be patient. After all, Rome wasn't built in a day.'

The lawyer added, as John reached the door, 'I'll write to Jones today,' as if this were a mark of extraordinary celerity and even special treatment.

The conversation with the lawyer did nothing to improve John's temper or assuage his impatience. He even thought of trying another lawyer, but common sense prevailed. They were probably all the same, these lawyers. But John's entrails felt as if they had been tied in knots.

Meanwhile, Felix continued to grow — physically. Actually, he became a nice little boy, most of the time, easily pleased and full of laughter at small things, if sometimes given to tantrums over equally small things. But he still needed a lot of attention, all the attention that Joanna could give. As for Henry, he took Felix's good nature as further proof of his terminal idiocy. When, for example, Felix laughed because a butterfly flew in at the window, Henry would say, 'What's funny about that, moron? Haven't you ever seen a butterfly before?'

Joanna feared that Henry was so contemptuous of Felix that he might one day do him harm. Indeed, once or twice (or more), Felix had bruises that were unlikely to have been caused merely by a fall — though admittedly he was very clumsy.

'Do you know how Felix got those bruises?' Joanna asked Henry, tying to make it sound like an enquiry rather than an accusation, though Henry was not deceived.

'No,' replied Henry angrily. 'Why should I? I'm not with Felix all the time, am I?'

One day, a policeman arrived at the door. He had come to warn Henry that, together with others, he had been seen trying to break into a car and that if he continued down this path… well, who knew what might be the result?

John and Joanna talked about it that evening. They each blamed the other.

'You spend all your time with Felix. You have no time for Henry,' said John.

'And you have no time for either,' said Joanna. 'You spend all your time going over law books.'

It was true that John spent a lot of time poring over books about the law of tort and spent the weekends trying to find relevant case reports. He had become very well-informed on the subject, as well as on birth injuries. He wanted to be ready for the next stage of proceedings.

'It's for Felix's sake,' he said. 'Don't forget that we're not going to live forever. He'll need someone to look after him.'

'Especially if I die before you,' said Joanna. She seemed unable to grasp the point that, unless they provided for Felix, he would have to go into the type of home about which scandals — ill-treatment, half-starvation — were always erupting in the press. And the only way, realistically, that they could provide for him was to win a big settlement.

'You're not doing it for Felix,' said Joanna. 'You're doing it for yourself. It's become your hobby. What's more, you're determined to prove yourself. It's got nothing to do with Felix anymore.'

John changed the subject.

'Anyway, what are we going to do about Henry?'

'I think we should take him to see somebody.'

'Who?'

'I don't know. A psychologist.'

After enquiries and a search on their computer, they found a psychologist nearby who specialised in the problems of children of Henry's age. They told Henry that they were going to take him to see her.

'What for? There's nothing wrong with me.'

But John and Joanna still had enough authority over him to take him whether he liked it or not.

The psychologist, a willowy woman in a bandanna and a faded cotton floral dress, spoke to Henry alone for an hour, having first spoken to them while leaving Henry to read in the wating room. At least he liked to read: there was nothing wrong with his intelligence when he cared to use it.

They took Henry to see the psychologist once more. This time she did not speak to the parents but only to Henry.

'What did she say to you?' they asked on their way home.

'Nothing. She made me do some silly tests.'

They couldn't get him to say anything more. Henry was very angry.

The psychologist sent John and Joanna a long report. Most of it consisted of what they had already told her.

'She has to justify her fee somehow,' said John.

After the repetition of what they had told her (it included a number of errors), the report contained a series of charts and graphs which showed how Henry scored on a number of traits such as extraversion and tendency to blame others, by comparison with other children of his age.

'What does she say in conclusion?' asked Joanna. 'Never mind all these graphs.'

'I'll read it,' said John.

In summary (it went), Henry is a boy who is entering adolescence earlier than his chronological age, who is of high intelligence but with a high degree of impulsivity, who feels neglected by comparison with his young sibling, and therefore has low self-esteem. He tries to compensate for this, and attract the attention of his parents, by conspicuous misbehaviour. Not only does this impact severely on his schoolwork such that his performance is much below his true potential and ability, but as he grows older and physically stronger, it could lead to serious conflict with the law. I therefore recommend that his parents rebalance the time they devote to caring for Henry's brother and the attention they pay to Henry. In that way, Henry's self-esteem will be restored, his schoolwork will improve, and his tendency to boost self-esteem by committing anti-social acts will diminish.

'Useless,' said Joanna. 'A complete waste of time and money.'

'But she's right,' said John. 'You hardly spend any time at all with Henry. It's all Felix, Felix, Felix, Felix. What can you expect? No wonder Henry feels the way he does. He'll grow up to be a criminal if this goes on.'

'And you? What do you do for Henry, you and your idiot lawbooks? What he needs is for you to do things with him, not to be an amateur lawyer.'

Their arguments went round and round like a wheel in a hamster's cage.

'I'm trying to get the hospital to pay compensation so that we can employ someone to look after Felix so that you can pay more attention to Henry.'

'That's not true. Henry'll be in prison by then.'

'Don't be melodramatic.'

'We've already had a visit from the police.'

The bad feeling between them persisted. All the same, John made an effort to do things with Henry — take him to the cinema, to the swimming pool, even to a football match — but Henry did not really want to be seen to do things with his father. His friends, some of whom had no fathers, thought it was babyish and mocked him for it.

'You see?' said John to Joanna. 'He needs you, not me.'

'It's because you've left it too late.'

'That's right, it's all my fault, blame it on me.'

'In this case, yes.'

They received an appointment from Professor Jones sooner than expected. The lawyer claimed to have twisted the professor's arm, though he did not specify the means he had supposedly employed.

The professor saw them both and examined Felix in his private clinic. It was very different from the hospital, where an atmosphere of incipient crisis was perpetual. Here, there was an atmosphere almost of monastic calm. The professor conducted his examination of Felix in front of John and

Joanna. He knew how to gain Felix's confidence and made him laugh merrily.

Afterwards, the professor was very non-committal: he would not be drawn into any rash statement, as if he might be held to account for any such. All he would say was that, yes, Felix was severely handicapped and would remain so for the rest of his life.

'But was it caused by the hospital?' asked John.

'I'll have to look at the records more closely,' said the professor. 'Then I'll send my report.'

The report took more than a month to arrive. The lawyer said that it was very favourable to 'our' case: that Felix's condition had been caused by a shortage of oxygen during birth was virtually certain. No other explanation was viable — would fly, as the lawyer put it.

John was exultant. He had been right to take the action. For the first time, John took Joanna with him to the lawyer's office.

'So you see,' John said to her in front of the lawyer, 'they won't be able to get away with it after all.'

The lawyer held up the palm of his hand like a policeman stopping traffic and advised caution.

'There's still some way to go,' he said. 'We're not home and dry yet. Jones' report is very good as to causation, couldn't be better, but don't forget that the other side will want its one expert report.'

'But the Professor is certain,' John said.

'Yes, but you can always find someone to contradict anything.'

'Facts are facts.'

'They always require interpretation. Nothing speaks for

itself. I think I mentioned to you that Jones has a sworn enemy in Davies.'

'You didn't.'

'Perhaps I should've done. Well, he has. If Jones says white, Davies says black, and vice versa.'

'But you did say that Jones was the best.'

'Oh yes, he is, I don't go back on that. He wins three quarters of his cases. But Davies is good.'

'I thought…'

'That's where the problem lies — one problem, at least. A bigger problem is that we now have to prove negligence, and that is always more difficult. I think we should have Pomeroy. He's very good, as good as Jones in his own field. He can turn cases around single-handed.'

'And he also wins three quarters of his cases?' asked Joanna.

'Yes, I should say so. At least.'

'So it's three quarters of three quarters,' Joanna said. 'That's just over a half.'

'I would put it at about seventy per cent,' said the lawyer imperturbably. 'I said three quarters for both of them, but that is a very conservative estimate. I should have said four fifths, perhaps, or even more. We lawyers are very cautious in what we say to our clients. It's our professional deformation, as the French say.' He came as near to laughing as he ever did.

'Will we have to take Felix to see this Pomeroy?' asked Joanna. 'It always disturbs him to be examined…'

'Oh no, he'll just work from the records. But as I said, being so good, he's also very busy. You have to remember that doing medico-legal reports is only a side-line for him.'

'A side-line?' said Joanna.

'I don't mean he's an amateur, or anything like that. On the contrary, he's the best, extremely professional. But he has a very busy practice, and naturally that has to come first. I mean, if you had a very sick child, you wouldn't expect a doctor to say, "I'll attend to him later because I have an urgent medico-legal report to complete," would you?'

'No,' said John, before Joanna could say anything.

'I'll write to Pomeroy today, but it'll probably be six months before we hear anything from him.'

John and Joanna had another argument on the way home.

'I told you it was all a waste of time,' she said.

'You heard him,' said John. 'He said the chances were seventy per cent. The alternative is zero per cent. It would be mad to give up now.'

'This is going to go on for years. You're obsessed by it.'

'It's our only hope.'

Henry began to truant from school. The first that John and Joanna heard of it was a letter they received from the schools inspector who informed them that Henty had missed school without explanation for six days of the last twenty. Not only would this adversely affect his education, wrote the inspector, but if it continued, his parents would face prosecution.

At first, John and Joanna were angry not at Henry but at the school inspector. How were they expected to keep Henry at school? That, surely, was the school's job. After all, Joanna duly delivered him to the school gates every morning and watched that he entered. If the school could not ensure that he attended properly, how could they? But after calming down a little, they both realised that they were missing the point. Henry was getting out of control.

They decided to speak to him together so that he could not play one of them off against the other. Unusually, they formed a united front. They sat Henry down at the table in the kitchen. He looked sullen and resentful at being treated in this way, so unjustly. Such a proceeding could bode him no good.

'We've had a letter from the school inspector,' said Joanna.

'So?' said Henry.

'He says that you've been truanting.'

'You mean, bunking off?'

'It doesn't matter what you call it. He says you've been missing from school six days out of the last twenty.'

'How does he know?'

'He knows, it's his job,' said John, as if everybody did his job.

'He can't know,' said Henry defiantly, 'because it's not true. And you can't know what's not true.'

'Don't lie,' said Joanna.

'How do you know?' said Henry, with all the anger of the justly accused. 'You weren't there.'

'Don't speak to your mother like that,' said John.

'Like what?'

'Go to your room!' demanded John.

'I can't, I'm meeting Nelson.' Nelson was his best friend and a bad influence, his father in and out of prison for drug-dealing.

Henry's parents were nonplussed. What could they do? In their hearts, they each blamed the other for the pass to which things had come.

'Anyway,' said Henry, reaching the door, 'it was only four, not six.'

Henry became more and more difficult. John again said that Joanna should pay less attention to Felix and more to Henry, but Joanna said that that was impossible. It was John's job, she said, to keep Henry out of trouble. He was a male, after all. Henry would soon be a man, too old to listen to a woman.

The lawyer phoned them to tell them that Pomeroy's report had come in unexpectedly early. He didn't want to disclose its content over the phone: he preferred to do so in person

'I'm afraid it's not very good news,' he said when they arrived and had settled on their chairs. 'Pomeroy doesn't support our case very strongly.'

'What does he say?' asked John.

'Well, he says that the records show that the hospital didn't really do anything wrong.'

'But they didn't know what they were doing,' protested John. 'That was obvious. They were flailing around for things they couldn't find. I mean, their panic… it proved it.'

'I'm sure you're right,' said the lawyer. 'Otherwise, I wouldn't have taken on the case.'

'So?'

'So our problem is that Pomeroy says that the records show than nothing was done or not done that was out of the range of normal practice. And that is the hurdle that we have to clear.'

'They must have altered the records or not written down all that happened.'

'That's quite possible. I spoke to Pomeroy and he agreed, but it would be difficult to prove. What is written down is often what ought to have been done rather than what was actually done.'

'There's our evidence,' said John. 'We could see that they didn't know what they were doing.'

'I'm afraid that an ounce of contemporaneous written records is worth a ton of verbal evidence — in strictly legal terms, I mean.'

'Where do we go from here?' asked Joanna.

'I'm sorry to have to advise you to drop the case.'

'Give up? But it's an open and shut case,' protested John.

'In your minds, yes, I agree, and perhaps in reality. But the law doesn't deal in truth. It determines who makes out the best case.'

'Pomeroy's not the only expert in the field,' said John. 'We could get another report.'

'Well, yes, we could,' said the lawyer. 'But there's a problem with that.'

'What's that?'

'Our insurance.'

'Insurance? What's that got to do with it?'

'You see, we can only take on cases like yours if we insure ourselves against losing.'

'But we haven't lost, we've only got Pomeroy's report. There are plenty of other fish in the sea.'

'Under the conditions of our insurance, we are allowed to commission only one expert opinion on any aspect of the case. If we commission more than one — if we go on a fishing expedition, to take up your piscatorial metaphor — our insurance becomes null and void.'

'And then?'

'And then the partnership becomes liable for the whole

costs of the case should we lose.'

John and Joanna looked at each other angrily, though each of them was angry at something different.

'Moreover,' resumed the lawyer, 'once our chances of winning are estimated at less than two thirds, our insurance becomes null and void. That is why I would advise you to drop the case, because we cannot continue it on the present terms.'

'This is outrageous,' said John.

'It's realistic, the way of the world, I'm afraid,' said the lawyer. 'Of course, you can continue the case at your own expense and risk, in which case I would be happy to continue to represent you. But we would need a down-payment in advance, and I have to warn you that the law is expensive.'

'How expensive?' asked John, Joanna looking even more angrily at him.

'Very,' said the lawyer. 'Pomeroy's report alone will be two thousand five hundred, though he hasn't sent his bill yet, which reminds me that I must ask him to do so before our insurance is withdrawn.' He wrote a note to himself to remind him. 'After the event, it's difficult to claim for expenses. Anyway, another report would cost at least as much. Despite being the best, Pomeroy's reasonable. Another expert might easily be three thousand or more.'

'We could afford that,' said John, Joanna shaking her head forcefully.

'Ah yes, but expert reports are the least of it, only a small proportion of the total. We have to charge more than their hourly rate, you see.'

'But that's dishonest,' said John. 'He's a professor.'

'He doesn't have our overheads. By the way, would you like

some coffee? I should have asked you before, I apologise.' Without waiting for an answer, he spoke to his secretary on the interphone, telling her to bring two coffees and some of those delicious biscuits.

'Not only my fees,' he resumed, 'but the court costs. Do you have any idea how much they are?'

They both shook their heads.

'Have a guess.' The lawyer's tone had unexpectedly turned playful, as if he were the compere of a TV quiz show.

'No idea,' said John.

'If the case came to court,' said the lawyer, adding in a lower tone that he thought it would because the other side would not give in easily, 'it would take at least three days of court time at thirty thousand a day.'

The lawyer took an evident pride or pleasure in shocking them by the expense of the law. The extravagant cost was a kind of proof of his own value and importance.

'We could take a second mortgage!' said John.

'You must be mad!' exclaimed Joanna, horrified.

'I wouldn't advise that,' said the lawyer. 'I must be quite frank. From the first, I was doubtful whether this action would succeed.'

'But you said we had a good case,' said John. 'Nothing has changed. If we had a good case then, we have a good case now.'

'The law is very precise. A good case in the abstract is no guarantee of success. Justice and law are not the same.'

John and Joanna left the lawyer's office. They were both fuming.

'The crook!' said John. 'He led me down the garden path.'

'It was your own fault. You wanted to be led down it. He saw you coming.'

'The hospital's going to get away with it scot-free.'

'I told you that would happen, but you wouldn't listen to me.'

'We mustn't let it.' He sounded like a thwarted boy who had stamped his feet. 'If it does, they'll ruin other people's lives just like they've ruined ours. We mustn't let that happen.'

'You're not to take a second mortgage,' said Joanna. 'Anyway, you can't, not without my approval. The house is in both our names, remember.'

John knew Joanna: she wouldn't change her mind whatever he said. He had reached the end of the legal route to the amelioration of their situation. Against his inclination, and for lack of any other possibility, he began to take a little more interest in Felix rather than in the case of Felix. For example, he would take him to the park when the weather was fine and he was able. He had never done that before, and he thought it would help Joanna to pay more attention to Henry. But he didn't enjoy it.

Instead, it only seemed to make things worse. Henry became even more insolent and defiant.

'Why does Dad keep taking It to the park?' asked Henry with a sneer. 'It's not as if either he or It enjoys it. It doesn't even know where it is.'

This wasn't true. Felix laughed and gurgled with pleasure whenever he saw a dog running on the grass or when he would chase a pigeon for a few yards. He clapped his hands and pointed happily as if the banal were extraordinary. He was living proof, said Henry, that little things please little minds.

John at first was torn between pleasure at seeing Felix's pleasure and irritation that he never progressed beyond the simplest things. It would be even worse as Felix grew older and the disparity between his mental and chronological age would become a yawning gulf. A lifetime of having to watch his son find waddling ducks hilarious! Felix would never be able to do up his own shoelaces. And that was quite apart from the terrible effect he was having on Henry. A lifetime of servitude to achieve nothing but Felix's survival!

John and Joanna now suspected that Henry was smoking dope. He would arrive home in a state of irritable torpor, the whites of his eyes reddened. He found whatever was said to him stupid, and he would either laugh or rage at it, according to swiftly changing mood. All he wanted was to be left alone to communicate with his disreputable friends by telephone. What had he to say to them? John and Joanna would have liked to know, but Henry clung to his telephone as a tyrant's bodyguard clings to a tyrant. Between their children's idiocy and sullenness, life was intolerable for John and Joanna.

In the park to which John now took Felix was a little lake. There were warning notices around it: Deep Water; Do Not Feed the Ducks; No Swimming; Fishing Forbidden. There was a wooden bridge in the Japanese style over the lake from which Felix liked to watch the ducks below. Sometimes there would even be a goose or a swan. When Felix saw one of these, he would clap his hands excitedly and say 'Wan!' Wan!' John would try to get him to say Swan, but it was beyond Felix's capabilities.

John would lift Felix up to get a clearer view of the birds. He would then hold him on the bridge's handrail. One day, the day after a policeman had called again about Henry's shoplifting, John lifted Felix as usual, and as Felix had wanted.

'Liff me! Liff me!' he had cried, as if it would be a new and exciting experience for him.

It had been raining hard the day before, and the water below, never clear, was turbid, like strong tea with milk. There were no ducks swimming in it, as if they were afraid of soiling themselves. The sky was still covered with rain-laden clouds, and there was no one around.

'Where quackers, where quackers?' asked Felix, looking down and seeing none.

'Look, over there!' said John, pointing to the farthest shore of the little lake. As he did so, he felt Felix wobble. At that moment, John saw the whole of his and Felix's life before him: years, decades of useless, thankless servitude. He withdrew the one hand that was holding Felix upright on the rail, and in a fraction of a moment he was gone, plunged into the water below. There was a splash, ripples and some bubbles.

John panicked. He ran down from the bridge to the shore of the lake below and waded in. The muddy bottom acted like suckers on his feet. He plunged further in, but it was useless: you couldn't make anything out in this water. John took out his telephone. Whom should he call? The police? An ambulance? The fire brigade?

Yes, that was it, the fire brigade. Breathlessly, he called them.

'There's been a terrible accident,' he said. 'My son's fallen into the water.' He was so distressed that he had difficulty in describing his precise location.

The firemen arrived a few minutes later. It didn't take them long to find Felix's body. One of them tried to console John, while another called the police and an ambulance. When the police arrived, one of the policemen said to John, 'I'm sorry, sir, you'll have to come with us to the station.'

'Can I call my wife first?' asked John.

'Of course, sir,' said the policeman, who listened carefully to what John had to say to his wife.

'Joanna,' he said, 'I don't know how to tell you. There's been a terrible accident. Felix slipped and fell into the water, and… and…' He broke down, unable to go on.

The policeman put his hand on John's shoulder.

'Come on, sir,' he said, not unkindly. 'We've got to go.'

John was taken to the police station where he was given a blanket to wrap round his wet lower legs and a cup of tea in a chipped enamel mug. He was asked to wait in a room without windows in which white polystyrene tiles absorbed all sound. There was a metal table in the room and three folding chairs. The light was bright.

After about a quarter of an hour, two policemen entered, only one of them in uniform.

'I'm Detective-Sergeant West,' said the one in civilian clothes, an ill-fitting black suit. 'And this,' he continued, pointing to his colleague, 'is PC Williams.' The latter was as expressionless as a piece of Utility furniture.

'Do you feel up to speaking to us?' asked DS West.

John nodded.

'First,' said the Detective-Sergeant, as if getting something unpleasant over with, 'we'd like to express our condolences for your tragic loss today. Don't we, Williams?'

'Yes, sir,' said Williams.

'Would you like to tell us what happened today?' said the Detective-Sergeant to John. 'Off the record.'

'I went to the park with Felix — he's severely handicapped, you know. I lifted him up on to the handrail of the bridge as usual to see the ducks. He's fascinated by ducks, he loves them. And then... and then...'

'Take your time, sir,' said the Detective-Sergeant.

'The rail was slippery because of the rain. He wriggled and broke free. And then... he... he...'

'I see. Then you waded into the lake and called the Fire Brigade who called us. Well, that seems fairly straightforward. Williams here will prepare a statement for you to sign. Of course, you need only sign it if it is a true statement of what happened. We don't want to put words into your mouth.'

The Detective-Sergeant left the room and PC Williams sat at the table to write the statement, writing on a form somewhat laboriously, in childish handwriting. When he finished, he asked John to read it through and sign it if it was an accurate record.

John read it, the words entering his eyes but hardly his mind. He signed all three pages of the statement, as did PC Williams as witness.

'We'll take you back home now, sir,' said PC Williams, gathering up the papers. 'Wait here,' he said, as if otherwise John might have gone wandering.

The Detective-Sergeant accompanied them back home. They were mostly silent: there was nothing to say. But halfway through the journey, the Detective-Sergeant let fall a single remark.

'Funny,' he said, 'there weren't any ducks on the pond

today.'

They reached home. John realised how much he had feared to do so. Under the eyes of the Detective-Sergeant, he tried to embrace Joanna, but she pushed him away. As the policemen left, the Detective-Sergeant said 'You'll be hearing from us after the postmortem. I must ask you not to leave the area.'

Joanna was angry and resentful as much as she was tearful.

'How could you have let him fall in?' she said — and nothing else. An ice-age descended on the house.

Henry took the news well, that is to say almost with a smile. Felix was no loss to the world.

Two days later, the Detective-Sergeant appeared again.

'I'm arresting you,' he said to John, 'on suspicion of murder. You don't have to say anything, but anything that you do say…'

John was handcuffed and led away. Apparently, bruises had been found on Felix's drowned body. Henry sometimes treated him very roughly.

John was asked whether he wanted a lawyer to be present during his police questioning, and if so who. The only lawyer John knew was the one who had represented him in the case against the hospital. He agreed, as for the time being there would be no need for a second mortgage. He advised John to say nothing to the police, not even to give his name — because, he said, once you start answering, you never stop.

John was taken to prison. There was no question of bail on so serious a charge. Everything around him was unreal, as if in a parallel, or dream, world. It was as if he were conscious and unconscious at the same time. Joanna did not visit him. Instead, she sent him the first papers of divorce proceedings.

The only person who came to visit him was the lawyer.

'Our defence that it was accidental won't fly,' he said. 'No jury will believe it. I advise you strongly against it.'

John looked at him. He might as well have been talking about something that had nothing to do with him.

'We'll have to go for mitigating circumstances — psychiatric. I'll get Toogood. He's marvellous in the box. I've known him to turn hopeless cases around.'

GHOST STORY

They had both reached the age at which reminiscence was the greatest pleasure left to them. After they had finished detailing their ailments — a growing list, with yet another joint added to the list in the competitive game of more-arthritic-than-thou — they settled down to the dissection of the past, both events and characters they had known. It was a particular joy to recall the sticky end to which a fellow-student of brilliant promise came, as if his failure somehow ameliorated the mediocrity of their own careers.

'Do you remember old…?'

He had had to flee the country after he had been caught with his fingers in the pie, and no one knew where he was or even if he were still alive — in Bolivia, perhaps.

They had both had a scientific training, and neither believed in ghosts. They had also lived without religious belief and were convinced that death was the end of it all, at least as far as they were concerned. They did not want to die, but at the same time they told each other that the thought of death no longer held any terrors for them. They had done in life all that they were ever going to do.

They spoke mainly by telephone, living as they did at some distance from each other. Occasionally, however, they would meet. If it was at one of their homes, a bottle of wine or more would oil and lengthen their conversations.

'Do you remember old…?'

'He was always a bit of a creeping Jesus.'

They remembered how he had worn a little metal fish on his lapel that indicated that he was among the Saved, the latter word used in a strictly technical sense for those who had accepted their Saviour into their hearts. Not only had the follies of youth found in him stony ground, but he left a trail of serenity after him as a snail leaves a trail on a paving stone.

'He was always smiling, because he knew that God loved him.'

'God even helped him in his exams.'

'It was hard work rather than divine intervention.'

'Yes, but he always prayed that he would be hard-working.'

'And he always wore a tweed jacket, even when he was twenty.'

'Some are born old, some achieve old age, and some have old age thrust upon them.'

It had to be admitted, though, that he had been successful. He had presumably taken his success as further proof of God's particular favour towards him. He would have interpreted any setbacks on the way to success as a testing by God or punishment for the sin of pride, a theological equivalent of what economists call a stress-test for banks, to see whether the bank could survive a collapse in the stock or property market.

'I'm sure he passed such tests without any difficulty.'

'His capital reserves in the Bank of God were always more

than adequate, sufficient to cover any emergency.'

'Do you remember how he would sidle up to people and ask them whether they wanted to be born again?'

'He asked me that once. I said to him, No thanks, once was quite enough. He never asked again.'

'You gave him a chance to turn the other cheek and to suffer for righteousness's sake. He should've been grateful to you.'

'He tried once to preach outside the faculty entrance.'

'I remember. There were about fifteen of us around him. He stood on some kind of wooden box. We didn't realise at first what he was doing. Then he started. "The Bible says there are three kinds of fool," he said. And Smithy called out, "Yes, and you're one of them." We all dissolved into laughter, and that was the end of his preaching career.'

'At least, to the unconverted. He continued, I believe, in that Nissen-hut church of his.'

'No, he had to give it up even there. I remember reading some years ago that there had been a scandal.'

'Where did you read it?'

'I think it must have been in Private Eye. It's the only publication that would have been interested in a story of sex, fraud and heresy in the World Church of Salvation, or whatever his hut was called.'

'I can't imagine him having been involved in sex and fraud.'

'Oh, but he was. If I remember, he held séances, which was a heresy in the church. He was expelled. There was some kind of investigation into the financial advice that the spirits had given him in his use of church funds. Nothing was ever really proved.'

They savoured their malicious pleasure for the moment, adding that he had had an affair with one of the mediums at his séances, leading to divorce.

'It didn't affect his career in any way.'

'He was very good at what he did.' This sounded almost as an accusation rather than as a compliment.

'Do you remember our own encounter with the au-delà?'

Neither of them believed in ghosts but had seen one once.

It was now fifty years ago, in the middle of their studies. One of them had lodgings in the garret of a large and neglected Victorian mansion which in the days of bourgeois prosperity had been the servants' quarters. The owners of the house, whoever they were, hoped that the house would fall into such a state of disrepair that it had to be demolished and the extensive, laurel- and rhododendron- filled gardens could be sold off for development, but for the moment the house was habitable enough for it to be the object of a preservation order by the city council.

Strangely enough, there had been a private chapel attached to the house, no longer in use, of course, except as a garage and depository of junk. You could still see shards of stained glass in the gothic windows that were mainly smashed, though some of the leading remained. By what process had this happened? Was it the hand of Nature or of Man that had done it, and if the latter, why? It was only fifty years later that the question occurred to them. As one ages, one takes the world less for granted. At the time, the destruction aroused no curiosity in them: it was just there. The world for them was what it was.

At night, the house was in dark. It was set back from the

road, and the light from the old-fashioned streetlamps did not reach it. A gravel drive led up to the front door and made a crunching sound underfoot that the producers of radio plays used to imitate to indicate the arrival of a character at a bourgeois or aristocratic house. Even fifty years ago, gravel drives were becoming rare: gravel was mostly asphalted over for the convenience of cars, all large houses in the city having been converted into flats or bed-sits, each occupant having a car that needed to be parked at night.

The large hall of the house was unlighted, as was the grand staircase that led up from it. There was a flat on the ground floor occupied by a lecturer in Assyriology, his wife a translator from the Hungarian, and who kept themselves very much to themselves. Their heavy, original Victorian door to their flat was so well-made that no chink of light emerged from it, also deadening any sound.

Only someone who had entered by day and had registered the lay-out of the hallway in his memory could find the stairs with ease at night. Everyone else had to hold his arms stretched out before him and advance gingerly, with tiny steps, for fear of bumping into or tripping over something. Such visitors — who were not many — would have thought, 'So this is what it is like to be blind!' The house was a lesson in true darkness, all the more unexpected in a city. Even those who were familiar with it by day had to feel their way as if in a game of blind man's buff, if they were not to miss the target of the staircase.

There was another hazard in ascending the staircase to the garret on the third floor: the tenant called Peter on the floor below. Peter could not have been his real name, because he came from East Bengal. He lived with his wife, so-called, an Irish woman in her thirties who was seldom seen but only glimpsed like a shy animal in a thick forest. Peter was very jealous: every man wanted her, and she wanted every man, so that the price of her fidelity was eternal vigilance. There were furious, one-sided rows in his flat, from which emerged a rich repertoire of insults and accusations, all of them palpably absurd, believable only as a prelude to violence. Everyone who ever heard one of these rows expected that Bridget would one day be murdered, Peter cutting up the body to dispose of it. He was the type who would.

What they lived on, nobody knew. Peter appeared to have no regular work, but it was difficult to imagine him in a social security or unemployment office, meekly complying with the rules and jumping through bureaucratic hoops just to receive a pittance. He was too hot-tempered for that: he would have exploded with rage at the first official obstruction or obduracy that he met. He stood on his dignity which he felt to be always under attack.

It did not help that he was very small, though he was spare and wiry and gave the same impression of strength as a ferret. His movements were swift and darting. You felt that if he wanted to stab you, it would all be over in a second, and there was nothing you could do to prevent it. If he wanted to kill you, he would.

Nor was it impossible that he would want to kill you, for he was volatile in the extreme, like nitroglycerine. Small things evoked in him huge rage: his anger was never proportional to what caused it, but always of the same intensity. He detested noise; at least, other people's noise. Of the noise he made himself, he was clearly more tolerant. As soon as he heard noise not his own, he rushed to the front door of his flat, his eyes flashing, and demanded silence. He screamed that he couldn't hear himself think because of the racket, which in truth might have been but a faint and short-lived sound, like the scaping of a chair on the floor above. His sensitivity to noise implied that he lived by intense thought, whose train could not be disturbed, though what he thought about no one could say. He threatened to call the police, though it was unlikely that his relations with that organization were very cordial.

Like many oversensitive people, Peter magnified the thing — in this case, noise — he was oversensitive to. At the sound of a footfall above, he would scream, 'Silence!'

Visitors to the garret said that they found Peter an amusing and interesting case, though they could not specify what he was a case of and really they were afraid of him, especially at night (and he seemed almost entirely nocturnal). His dark skin made him especially suited to night-time attack in such a house. They approached and left the garret on tiptoe. It was like being on the edge of a volcano that could erupt at any time.

Once, when the two of them had been together with two girls and their laughter had been all-too audible to Peter, he came banging on the door. There he stood, his hair wild, his eyes flashing, a large and viciously serrated knife at his side.

'Are you running brothel?' he demanded to know.

They were young, and the young are afraid to appear afraid.

'Are brothels noisy, then?' one of them said. 'I suppose you must know.'

'Cheeky young devil!' said Peter, raising his knife and waving it a little. 'Keep your noise down. Some of us have to sleep. We have to go to work.'

Peter had never been seen to go to, or come from, work, but this was not the moment to point it out: even though young, with a taste for verbal provocation, they knew that they had reached a limit. The whites of Peter's eyes, normally a striking contrast with the darkness of his complexion, were bloodshot: he had been drinking.

'Next time I hear…' he said, agitating his knife and then retreating down the stairs.

They were subdued afterwards. It was not much fun with a murderous lunatic below who was ready to cut throats.

A few weeks later, the two of them shared a bottle or two of wine. Passing the lair of the wild beast without arousing him always lent a sense of achievement to a visit, making visits elsewhere unexciting by comparison. Peter's existence added a certain interest to life, which he saved from the curse of banality, as danger often does.

They were still of an age when philosophical questions seemed of the first importance and before it occurred to them that they would not be able to solve the questions that had puzzled mankind for millennia. They were young men of good but not exceptional abilities, and their lives would continue on their courses whatever answer they gave to those questions. They discussed the matter of determinism and free will as if their life depended on it and as if no one had ever discussed it before. Each would argue one side or the other and then suddenly switch sides, as if only for the mental exercise, as puppies or kittens play with rolls of paper or balls of wool.

Their discussion had lasted two or three hours and was now guttering like a candle. The wine had befuddled them a little, and they did not recognise their incoherence.

'Let's go for a walk,' one of them said.

'Good idea, but we'll have to be careful of Peter.'

They sidled down the stairs with almost thespian care, as if what counted was the effort they made rather than the effect they had. It was the early hours of the morning, when Peter's wrath tended to be at its most volcanic.

It was a moonless, overcast night. Older men than they might have felt the damp and the cold. They walked for about twenty minutes to clear their heads. There was a mist or fog falling. The visitor to the garret said that he would accompany his friend back to the house and then go home, it being the early hours of the morning and there being lectures to attend in a few hours' time.

Their heads were almost clear now, or so they thought. They had exhausted their desire to talk and walked silently, apart from the faint sound of their feet on the ground. The visitor remembered that he had bought a couple of books with him that he wanted to retrieve from the garret and, though he was unlikely to need them straight away and to retrieve them would risk provoking Peter, logic and impulse mix ill with youth (impulse always winning), and he insisted on retrieving them.

They turned into the gravel drive, which crunched underfoot, a pleasant sound. They were about thirty yards from the front door of the house; they could make out the laurels as a darker shade of black. They stopped in their tracks.

'Did you see something just now?' one of them asked the other.

'I thought I saw a man in a white cassock with a black cape pass in front of the house.'

'So did I.'

Though in the shape of a man, what they saw had glided rather than walked, and dissolved into the mist. It made no sound.

'It must have been the fog,' one of them said, but neither of them really believed it. The fact that they had both seen the same thing was against it.

Although it remained on their minds for some time afterwards, they agreed by that silent, mutual agreement between friends that needs no compact to speak of it no further. They each feared to appear foolish in the eyes of the other, a fear much stronger than any attachment to truth. They agreed, tacitly, that it was a non-subject between them.

Fifty years later, while talking again of old …, who had gone in for spiritualist heresy, fraud and sexual misdemeanour, and been expelled for it, one of them asked, 'Do you remember the time when…'

'I know what you're going to say,' said the other.

'The man who flitted across the front of the house and disappeared into the mist.'

It was as if they had spent the intervening half-century thinking about it. They hadn't done so, of course, but neither had they forgotten it, at least not in the sense of being unable to recall it. Their memory of it, if they called it up, was as vivid as ever.

'We were drunk at the time.'

'You don't see things just because you're drunk. It wasn't delirium tremens.'

'We'd stopped drinking.'

'You only get DTs after a long bout of heavy drinking. We liked a drink, but we never got to that stage.'

'Perhaps you imagine things when you've been drinking.'

'But not the same things in the same place at the same time. After all, I asked you what you'd seen without telling you what I'd seen.'

'But you said, or implied, that you'd seen something.'

'Yes, but I didn't say what. It could have been anything. Instead, you saw exactly what I saw.'

'It could have been a coincidence.'

'Ha! What were the chances of that?'

'It's impossible to say. If you don't know the initial conditions, you can't work out the likelihood of any coincidence happening.'

'All the same, nothing like it has happened to me before or since.'

'How many events are there in a human life?'

'Impossible to calculate.'

'At any rate a huge number, let us say for the sake of argument a thousand a day. That's three hundred and sixty-five thousand events a year. In seventy years, that's about twenty-five million. Is it conceivable that in such a life that there should be no coincidences? That would be the greatest coincidence of all.'

'I think you're whistling in the wind. You don't want to think about the meaning of what we saw.'

'What does it mean? Don't tell me that just because you've

reached the age of seventy that you've started to believe in life after death!'

'I'm only wondering what it means or meant, that's all. You can't deny the experience itself.'

'Consider the condition we were in. We'd been drinking. We were tired. There was a mist swirling around. We'd run the gauntlet of Peter. We were in a state of heightened suggestibility.'

'I still come back to the coincidence, as you call it, of having seen the same thing.'

'There are many possible explanations. Perhaps there really was a person who walked across the front of the house like that.'

'We both knew at the time that it wasn't just a normal man. He appeared out of nothing and disappeared into nothing.'

'That's how things are in thick mists.'

One of them thought the other had gone a little soft in the head while the other thought that the rigidity of old age had sent in. Their friendship was too old, though, for any mere disagreement to spoil it. They changed the subject.

A few months later, one of them received through the post a newspaper cutting in a letter from the other:

Mystery of 120-year-old murder solved

It seemed that a Dominican monk, lodging temporarily in the house, had been poisoned with arsenic, but no culprit had been found. The monk had been a convert, which had enraged his family (such things were taken seriously in those days), and an old diary, written by his brother, had been found in an old store cupboard. His brother fulminated against the Antichrist in the family, who was a heretic of the worst kind.

It was not right that he should continue to live and spread his popish superstition. He had thought of a way to dispose of him…

The sender of the cutting phoned its recipient.

'What do you think now?' he asked.

'What do I think now? I think beliefs are dangerous. You should avoid them.'

·